"What I Really Want To Know Is If There's A Man In Your Life Right Now."

He leaned closer and ran a finger across her bare left hand. "Looks like there's no husband. Is there a lover?"

Wrath gathered in Stacy's green eyes. "I don't believe this! Even you aren't this thickheaded. What on earth gives you the right to ask me a question like that?"

"Because I intend to be the next man in your life."

She stared at him, speechless. When she finally gathered her wits, she shook her head, holding out her hand like a cop stopping traffic. "Oh, no. No. Wrong. I'm only going to be here for a week. Less, if I'm lucky. You are definitely not on my list."

"Write me in." The three words were slow and sexy and raised the temperature in the truck about fifteen degrees.

Dear Reader,

Another year is drawing to a close here at Silhouette Desire, and I think it's a wonderful time for me to thank all of you—the readers—for your loyalty to Silhouette Desire throughout the years. Many of you write letters, letters that we try to answer, telling us all about how much you like the Desire books. Believe me, I appreciate all of the kind words, because let's be honest ... without *you*, there wouldn't be any *us!*

In the upcoming year we have many sexy, exciting stories planned for you. *Man of the Month* is continuing with books by authors such as Diana Palmer, Joan Hohl, Ann Major and Dixie Browning. Ann Major's SOMETHING WILD series is continuing, as is Joan Hohl's BIG BAD WOLFE series. We will have special "months of men," and also duets from authors such as Raye Morgan and Suzanne Simms. And that's just part of the Desire plan for '94!

This month, look for a wonderful *Man of the Month* title from BJ James. It's called *Another Time, Another Place,* and it's a continuation of her stories about the McLachlan brothers. Don't miss it!

So once again, thank you, each and every one of you, the readers, for making Silhouette Desire the great success that it is.

Happy holidays from

Lucia Macro
Senior Editor ... and the rest of us at Silhouette Desire!

RITA RAINVILLE
TUMBLEWEED AND GIBRALTAR

SILHOUETTE *Desire*®
Published by Silhouette Books
America's Publisher of Contemporary Romance

SILHOUETTE BOOKS

ISBN 0-373-05828-4

TUMBLEWEED AND GIBRALTAR

RITA RAINVILLE

has been a favorite with romance readers since the publication of her first book, *Challenge the Devil*, in 1984. More recently, she won the Romance Writers of America Golden Medallion Award for *It Takes a Thief*.

Rita has always been in love with books—especially romances. In fact, because reading has always been such an important part of her life, she has become a literacy volunteer and now teaches reading to those who have yet to discover the pleasure of a good book.

To Jill Marie Landis, Suzanne Forster and
Lori Herter. You know why.

One

"Oboy."

The single word was a whisper that fell somewhere between a groan and a plea.

Stacy Sullivan knew trouble when she saw it.

No one in the small town of Prudence, Kansas, had been better at spotting it. Or, for that matter, had had as much practice dealing with it. And neither time nor geography had dulled her senses, Stacy decided with a resigned sigh. Even on a godforsaken stretch of mountain road in northwestern Arizona, it looked exactly the same.

The snarling pickup truck that slid to a stop beside her dead car was big and dark beneath its coat of red dust and mud.

It looked aggressive.

And impatient.

Just like the man who stepped out, slamming the door behind him. Only he added an extra sense of danger to the picture. He was big, broad shouldered and lean hipped, wore faded jeans and moved with the grace and speed of a predator. His blue work shirt was partially unbuttoned with the sleeves rolled up his forearms, leaving little to the imagination. He was very tan and had lots of springy hair that was either dark brown or black on his chest, on his arms and beneath his wide-brimmed hat. He covered the distance between them in a couple of ground-eating strides.

Stacy muffled a groan and closed her eyes behind the dark lenses of her sunglasses. Her Aunt Tabby would have taken one look at the formidable man, fanned herself excitedly with a folded newspaper, sighed and said, "Oh, my, is he a sight, or what?" It was the all-purpose question that covered a multitude of situations. And sins. And Stacy, much against her will, had to agree.

He was a sight.

She took a quick, deep breath and tried to remember the instructions in the book of quickie meditations she had just bought. If ever she needed to be calm and centered, she had a feeling that now was the time. The look of taut control on the man's dark face gave her an even stronger feeling that she would need all the help she could get.

She took another deep breath and let it out slowly, remembering to count to five as she exhaled. She didn't even get to three.

"Lady, what the hell are you doing?" he demanded.

Stacy forgot all about counting. Oh, yeah, she decided, expelling the rest of the air from her lungs in a rush, he was definitely trouble. His voice was deep and rough around the edges, with more than a bit of impatience.

Opening her eyes, she blinked up at him thoughtfully. Way up. Sitting cross-legged on the hood of her shiny, new red car probably put her at a disadvantage, she reflected, but after another assessing glance she knew it wouldn't have made any difference where she was. He was at least six-four, which put him almost a foot taller than her five foot, five inch frame.

He was intimidating, and the only reason she wasn't scrambling for cover was because Long John, the friendly trucker she'd been talking with on the CB when her car died, had carefully described both the man and the truck he would send to help her.

Stacy gave him a tentative smile. "You're Gibraltar, I presume." His CB handle was apt, she reflected when he nodded. The man wasn't just a piece of the rock, he was the whole darn thing.

"And you're Tumbleweed." It was more statement than question, and the deep voice sounded resigned. When she nodded, thinking that the name she'd adopted was equally appropriate, he demanded again, "What are you doing, sitting up there?"

Stacy patted the warm metal beneath her and raised questioning brows. "Here? Meditating." Ignoring his astounded look, she said, "I didn't know how long it would take you to get here, so I thought I'd sit in the fresh air and relax."

Of course, Stacy admitted silently, she hadn't yet reached the point in the meditation process where it was anything but work, but the book said that practice was the only way to achieve that desired state of tranquillity. The book also said in the first few pages of chapter one—which was as far as she had gotten—that you didn't need any fancy equipment, just peace and quiet. And since her car had chosen to drop dead on a road brimming with precisely those two qualities, it had been the obvious place to give it another try.

After all, she reminded herself with a pleased sense of accomplishment, meditation was just one of the things she planned to incorporate in her new, exciting life-style in California. Everyone in that part of the country—at least those she had read about—agreed that meditation helped balance the pressures of life in the fast lane. Once she licked that, she could tackle the next project on her lengthy list. Each step closer to the new image was a step away from the staid and dull Ms. Sullivan she had left behind in Prudence.

"Let me get this straight." The big man, Gibraltar, gazed down at her with the expression a scientist might give a mutated lab specimen. "You're sitting out here, at noon, in the July sun, without a hat, to *relax?*"

Stacy nodded, momentarily distracted by the feel of her hair brushing her cheeks, then sliding back into place. It had just been two weeks since the stylist had given her a snazzy new haircut that looked like a sleek brown cap. Another thing she'd left behind in Prudence was the long hair that she'd worn knotted at her nape for the past six years.

He scowled. "Lady, the sun up here is almost as potent as it is in the desert. You're courting a heat stroke sitting there." He cast an assessing glance at the distant clouds and turned back to her. "And it won't be long before you'll be a sitting duck for a lightning bolt."

Stacy tried another smile, brighter this time, reminding herself that he had stopped doing whatever people did up here to come to her rescue. "My name is Stacy

Sullivan, not 'lady,' and I'm very grateful for your help."

"Evan McClain. Call me Mac." Ignoring the hand she held out for him to shake, he wrapped both of his large hands around her waist and lifted her as if she weighed no more than a hummingbird.

Stacy gasped and grabbed his shoulders. "Mr. McCl—"

"Mac."

"All right. Mac. Put me do—" She stopped when her feet touched the ground, her sandals and bare toes looking absurdly vulnerable next to his scuffed boots. Cowboy boots—with heels and pointy toes, she noted absently as he stepped around her and popped open the hood of the car—not the flat, laced boots preferred by the men she had known all of her life.

She blinked thoughtfully, taking in his overwhelming masculinity, his muscular thighs and lean hips, watching as he braced his hands on the car and stared down at the tangle of coils and wires. No, indeed, she thought wryly, we're not in Kansas anymore. In Prudence, those snug jeans would have been banned by the ladies' guild and all the churches.

"What happened?"

Stacy dragged her eyes away from shoulders wide enough to block the sun. "Hmm?"

"The car. What did it do?"

"It died."

"*Before* it died."

Moving beside him, Stacy stared down in frustration at the innards of the car. The new, shiny innards. The new, shiny innards that were guaranteed to work. She shrugged. "I don't know. One minute everything was fine. Then the whole dashboard lit up and the car rolled to a stop."

"Did it make any noise?"

She shook her head. "Not a sound. It just—"

"Rolled to a stop." Mac gave a sharp sigh. "Okay, we'll tow it into the ranch and take it from there."

Stacy backed up, wincing when he slammed the hood down. "Uh, can't we just take it into town? That way, I'll be out of your hair and—"

"Which town? The one a hundred miles back there—" he jerked a thumb over his shoulder "—or the one just as far that way?" He nodded to his right. "We're fifteen miles from the ranch, so the ranch it is. God knows we've got plenty of room."

"But I can't just—"

"Where are you from?" he asked abruptly.

Eyeing him with suspicion, Stacy said slowly, "Kansas."

"Big city?"

"Small town."

"And what would the folks in—"

"Prudence," she volunteered when he hesitated.

"Prudence do if they came across a woman whose car had broken down a hundred miles from nowhere? Leave her there?"

Stacy didn't even have to think about it. Her neighbors, while conservative—many of them twenty years behind the times and not too thrilled with a woman running the largest business in town—were good people and would never let a woman in trouble fend for herself.

She gave a sigh that held more than a bit of self-disgust. "You're right, of course. The ranch it is. And, Mac...thank you."

He shrugged and gave the car an appraising glance. "No problem."

"Look," she said worriedly, "would it be easier if I just grabbed a few things for the night and leave the car here? We could call a tow tru—" She stopped with a gasp when he extended a large hand and plucked her sunglasses from her nose. Black, she thought. His hair was black, blue black, thick and a bit shaggy; long enough in back so it almost brushed his collar. He examined her rounded eyes and nodded as if he had just won a bet with himself. After settling her glasses back in place, he reached out and opened the truck door for her.

"Hop in, green eyes."

"Mac, I'm just trying to—"

He swung her up onto the high seat and slammed the door. Gazing down at her through the open window, he said calmly, "I know. But you don't have to. Just like I said, Stacy, it's no problem."

And that part wasn't. It took less than three minutes to attach the shiny red car to the pickup's tow bar.

No problem?

Who was he kidding?

Mac tightened his hands on the steering wheel and shot an oblique glance at Stacy. She was sitting, legs folded beneath her Indian style, in the impossible position that only women could seem to manage. She was gazing out the window, apparently absorbed in the rolling hills of the long valley. At least that's what it looked like, but it was hard to tell with half her face hidden by the dark glasses.

She had become a problem before he'd even hit the brakes and turned off the ignition. All it had taken was one glimpse of her.

It wasn't unusual to pick up a call for help on the CB; in this neck of the woods it was done all the time. He had lost count of the tourists who'd become stranded on the mountain roads. Normally whoever picked up the call played John Wayne.

The first inkling he'd had that this case was different was the concern in the trucker's rough voice and the fact that Long John wouldn't give out Tumbleweed's location until he talked to Gibraltar. From what Mac gathered, the trucker had fussed over her like a mother hen, wanting to turn around and get her himself, but she had told him she trusted his judgment. If Gibraltar was the local man he wanted to call, then she would wait for Gibraltar.

When he'd caught up with Mac, Long John's normally laconic voice had been tight with anxiety. Words had tumbled out over the CB—a waif from the Midwest heading for California. Sweet as a newborn babe. Poor kid didn't have a family to watch over her. She had been talking to truckers ever since she'd left home, and they had more or less taken her under their wings. Gibraltar had to help her, *now!* So he'd dropped the barbed wire he'd been using to repair a fence, driven like a bat out of hell down a twisting, turning road, expecting to find a terrified kid.

And what had he found?

Mac slanted another look at her. Stacy had on orange walking shorts and a green blouse that was tied at her midriff. Both were splashed with a wild print in blinding colors. He realized with a jolt that until that second he hadn't even noticed her outfit. He had been too damned busy looking at her.

She wasn't tall, at least not compared to him. The top of her head just reached his shoulder. He estimated she was in her late twenties, six or seven years younger than his own thirty-four years. Her hair was a glossy brown cap that made him want to thread his fingers through the silky strands. It picked up gold and red highlights from the sun and framed her face, swirling in a teasing cloud when she turned her head, then sliding effortlessly back into place. It also revealed her nape, a delicate, vulnerable curve that tempted him to trace it with his fingers, down her elegant spine to the lush curve of her bottom. His body stirred at the thought. Annoyed, he tromped on the gas pedal and shot the big truck down the road.

She wasn't beautiful. She was...cute, he decided. Behind the oversize sunglasses, her wide green eyes were tilted up at the corners, giving her the soft look of a curious kitten. Her nose was pert, with a scattering of freckles, and her mouth soft. Very soft.

He could handle it. He could cope with cute, Mac thought grimly. At least until her car was fixed and she was on her way to California or wherever she was heading. It had been too long since he'd had a woman in his life, but *cute* wasn't what he was looking for. Now that his house was on schedule and almost finished, it was time to start looking for a woman.

Not just any woman, he automatically reminded himself. *The* woman. The one who would be the perfect ranch wife and mother. One who would help forge a dynasty. The rare woman who would be content surrounded by tall mountain peaks and hard men, who would help him plant deep family roots and take pleasure in the passing seasons and years.

No, he told himself again, *cute* wasn't even in the running.

Deliberately shifting his thoughts from the softly scented woman next to him, he concentrated on the truckers. How had so many of them fallen under her spell? And how had they gotten the idea that she was barely out of school?

It stood to reason that none of them had ever seen her. They couldn't have, because even before he'd brought the pickup to a stop, seeing her perched on the car like a hood ornament—meditating, for God's sake—he'd known two things about her.

She wasn't the least bit scared.

And she wasn't a kid.

A bank of gray, fast-moving clouds covered the sun, and Stacy took off her dark glasses and stashed them in her shoulder bag. "So," she said brightly, turning away from the tumble of piñon and juniper framing the road to gaze at him. "How did Long John find you so fast? Frankly, I thought it would be hours before you got out here."

Mac shrugged. "I was in the barn and had the radio on."

Stacy grinned. "I must be leading a charmed life. Ever since I left Kansas, I've had guardian angels falling all over themselves to help me."

His brows rose. "The CB?" he guessed.

"Umm-hmm. I bought it just to have it on hand for emergencies." She leaned back against the door, adjusting the seat belt. "You know, like—"

"Like now," he said dryly.

She nodded. "Right. But the salesman suggested that I try it out several times so I'd know what I was doing, and the first time I did, I met the nicest trucker. His name was Colorado Joe."

Mac groaned.

"What?"

"Nothing."

"*What?*" She tilted her head, staring at his profile. "Oh, for heaven's sake," she said in disgust. "I'm not a child, and I'm not stupid. I know when someone's making a move on me. The man was *nice*. Lonely."

Mac grinned. "Sure."

Stacy exhaled noisily. "He just wanted to talk, all right?"

"Right."

Glancing at him suspiciously, she said, "Anyway, he explained how I should use the radio and introduced me to some of the other truckers." Before Mac could say a word, she added hastily, "They were perfect gentlemen. All of them. And good company for someone traveling alone."

Mac stared straight ahead. They were also the biggest gossips in the world. By now, probably half the truckers in the country knew about the woman called Tumbleweed. He lifted a shoulder in an impatient gesture. Fine. So they were friendly. And if she wanted to believe in the Tooth Fairy, that was also fine. Because he wasn't into *cute*, he reminded himself. She wasn't his problem. At least, not once her car was fixed.

"How'd you pick the handle?" he asked with casual curiosity.

Stacy's lips curved in a small, private smile that told him he was going to hear only what she wanted to reveal. And that wasn't going to be much, he decided, narrowing his eyes.

"Because that's exactly what I am." She almost purred in satisfaction. "I have no roots, nothing to tie me down, and that's exactly the way I want it. As the old song says, I'm 'drifting along with the tumbling tumbleweed.'" She sang the words softly. When he didn't respond, she looked at him inquiringly. "What about Gibraltar?"

"My friends came up with it. I suppose," he said finally, "it's because I'm slow and as big as a rock."

Stacy doubted that very much. Big? Yes, she'd grant him that, but there was nothing remotely slow about the man before her. If she had to venture a guess, it would be that neither reason applied. Mac McClain seemed a lot like the huge boulders along the road, dug in deep and not about to move. She would bet the company she no longer owned that he was deliberate, rock-solid reliable and not easily swayed. All in all, he was a man to depend on—probably until hell froze over—and the very last one she wanted to get involved with.

As far as that went, she didn't want *any* man. What she wanted was exactly what she had—freedom. Plus what she would find in California—the time and place to be different, to experience new, rare and exotic things. To bloom. And, as those in the fast lane would say, to find herself.

She had given away her trusty briefcase and business suits and bought jazzy little outfits perfect for mingling with people who lived on the cutting edge. And just for good measure, she had purchased an armload of books on meditation and discovering the exciting new woman within. She would learn to be a free spirit if it killed her, she told herself grimly, and she'd do it *now*. Or at least, she amended carefully as she straightened her legs, before she reached California.

And she would do it. Stacy didn't doubt that for a minute. She had learned the hard way how much could be accomplished by perseverance and determination. And now, those same qualities—the very ones that had helped assure her elderly relatives of an old age free from financial worries—gave her another kind of freedom. And she was going to milk it dry. Her pleased chuckle drew Mac's attention.

"You look like a cat with cream all over its whiskers."

She smiled, knowing that she probably did. Thoughts of freedom and adventure had that effect on her. "That's exactly how I feel."

Mac's sideways glance at her was almost his undoing. Swearing, silently and crudely, he righted the drifting truck, concentrating on keeping it on the road while he dealt with the shock jolting through him.

What the hell had happened to cute?

Stacy sat beside him, savoring a private thought—and sending sensual vibrations that would stun a bull elephant. Her smile was small, completely feminine, utterly contented, and satisfaction radiated from her in waves. Green eyes flashed behind the screen of her lowered lashes, issuing an invitation that would have appalled her if she had been aware of it.

That's what she would look like after she made love, eyes gleaming with contentment, a soft smile curving her lips.

Mac shifted at the thought, cursing blackly at the tension building between his thighs. The fact that she hadn't deliberately provoked it didn't make it any easier. On the contrary. He was thirty-four and had learned to control his hormonal reactions years ago. At least, he thought he had. The fact that a glimpse of her smile had sent his body into a full-fledged red alert not only stunned him, it annoyed the hell out of him. Much more of it and he'd have to drop his hat in his lap before he gave Stacy Sullivan the shock of her small-town life.

And it didn't matter a tinker's damn that she wasn't the kind of woman he was looking for. That she wasn't ranch material, wife material or dynasty material. He didn't care. He wanted to scoop her up and take her home. Not just for a night's refuge, not just as a polite host. To his bedroom. To his bed. Where he could watch her gorgeous eyes darken with the same hunger he was feeling. Where she'd melt all over him like warm honey, and he wouldn't be able to tell where he ended and she began.

Whoever she was, whatever she was, wherever she came from, he wanted her with a need and urgency he hadn't felt for years. If ever.

He wanted her.

Now.

Two

"I still think I should call for a tow truck from your place and ride into town. That way I—"

"I told you I have four empty bedrooms."

He had indeed told her, Stacy reflected, darting an assessing look at the big man beside her. Several times. And each time, his profile had gotten stonier and his voice grimmer. The man was stubborn beyond belief. She was offering him a graceful way out of what had suddenly become an awkward situation, and if he had any sense, he'd jump at it.

It was obvious that Mac didn't want her company any more than she wanted to face another Kansas tornado—or to inflict herself on a reluctant host. Stacy fixed her unblinking gaze on the broken yellow line running down the center of the road, considering the word. Reluctant? Yes, definitely.

If he had first stepped out of his truck feeling that way she would have understood; people had a tendency to be cranky when they were pulled away from their work. But he hadn't. His initial reaction had ranged from astonished disbelief to amused tolerance, with a hefty dose of masculine appreciation thrown in for good measure. And there had been enough of the latter to make her distinctly uneasy. Then in a blink of an eye, something had happened and he'd turned into a block of ice.

And now he was barreling down the road, determined to do the right thing. A code of the West thing, she decided. It probably came with the pointy-toed boots: take care of the little lady, even if you'd rather be bitten by a rattler. Or one of those weird, prehistoric-looking gila monsters.

Stacy allowed herself a small shrug and eased back in the seat. The cowboy had a problem. And while she was grateful for the rescue and appreciated the time and effort spent in her behalf, it was not her problem. She might never know what caused him to congeal behind the steering wheel, but six years in the corporate world had taught her that these things happened. And when they did, it was no use taking them personally. His withdrawal undoubtedly had nothing to do with her, she lectured herself briskly. Absolutely nothing at all.

Even so, the problem—whatever it was—did exist, and the best way she could show her gratitude was by getting out of his way and letting him deal with it. Fortunately for her, she had the means to do just that. Barely aware that he had turned off the main road, Stacy considered her options.

Staying at his ranch was definitely not one of them.

No, as soon as they arrived, she would call for a tow truck. It didn't matter how long it took; she would wait. It didn't matter how much it cost; she could afford it.

Leaving would solve another problem. A sticky one. Mac was... very male. Closing her eyes in disgust, she thought that as understatements went, that one ranked right up there with the best of them. Mac McClain was more than that. Far more. He might be the local Rock of Gibraltar and an upstanding member of the community, but he was still a renegade. He was a man who undoubtedly had fathers of unmarried daughters contemplating locked bedroom doors and shotguns—and the daughters learning to pick locks. He practically vibrated with sexual energy. And the fact that he kept it under tight control made him even more dangerous, not less.

Especially to a woman with dreams.

Living—or existing—celibate as she had for the past four years had left her vulnerable to a man like Mac. Stacy acknowledged the fact and accepted it as she had so many others; it was simply something to be dealt with. In Prudence, men like Mac had not only been in short supply, they had been nonexistent. But a lack of experience was no excuse for stupidity, she reflected, darting an oblique glance at his chisled profile. And that was exactly what it would be if she stayed in his house, even for a few days. Sharing the cab of the pickup for the last twenty minutes had taught her that much. Even iced over he sent out enough raw energy to light up a small town, and she knew her defenses were as inadequate as her diminishing supply of small talk. The last few years had taught her a lot, but not how to cope with a man like Evan McClain.

So, since she was neither stupid nor a masochist, she would leave. She had been free for exactly sixteen days, and no one—especially a broad-shouldered, lean-hipped, hungry-eyed cowboy—was going to ruin her plans.

The truck jolted to a stop and Mac turned to face her. "We're here. Home."

Wondering how soon she could get to a telephone, Stacy nearly missed the note of satisfaction in his voice. But the pride and possession were palpable, almost preparing her as she glanced out of the window.

Almost.

"Oh, my." Not waiting for him to come around to her side, Stacy pushed open the door and slid to the ground.

It was a far cry from the sun-faded, utilitarian structure she had expected, Stacy reflected, gazing at the gracious two-story house. Dazzling white with green shutters, it stood serenely on a knoll amid a tangle of piñon, juniper and ponderosa pines. Sunlight broke through the clouds for a long moment, dancing and reflecting on the sparkling windows. A white picket fence with a swinging gate neatly enclosed the lush grass and the path meandering down to the driveway.

"It's a pampered lady." Smiling, her gaze followed the rail of the wraparound porch before moving up to the gabled roofline. "And huge." And it did everything but dip, curtsy and break into a welcoming two-step.

"Fifteen rooms, counting all the bathrooms," he said complacently.

All it lacked was a garden, she decided, instantly picturing cascades of wisteria covering the latticed walkway at the side of the house. Masses of lilacs softened the corners, and sweetpeas twined through the picket fence. Clusters of top-heavy, lavender foxglove bloomed on either side of the porch stairs, flanked by rows of gladiolas and day lilies. And petunias, of course. Tons of colorful, flirting petunias.

Blinking away the picture, Stacy momentarily forgot her self-imposed lecture that she had to leave. She reached out to grab Mac's hand and tugged, heading for the gate. "Come on, I've got to see the rest of it. Who built it? How long have you had it? Where do you keep the elves who come out at night and paint everythi—"

"Mac?" A small, compact woman wearing purple jeans and a hot-pink shirt shoved open the screen door. Her short, curly hair was snowy white. "Curly needs you down at the barn. Pronto!"

Letting the door slam behind her, she trotted down the stairs in their direction, the heels of her ornate pearl gray boots thudding on the wooden treads. By the time she met them at the gate, she had assessed Stacy from head to bare toes. Approval gleamed in her snapping blue eyes. " 'Bout time," she said obscurely.

Mac's eyes narrowed in warning. "Maxie, this is Stacy Sullivan. Her car broke down, and she'll be staying here until it's fixed. Stacy, Maxie Dillard. She keeps the house running. She's so used to giving orders, she thinks she runs the place."

Maxie snorted. "Doesn't matter to me if you go or stay. Next time Curly hollers, I'll tell him to take care of the black foal himself, since you don't—"

"What's the matter with it?" Mac scowled down at her.

"That's why he's hollering," she said patiently. "So you'll go down there and—"

"Get Stacy settled," he ordered, running his hand through his thick, dark hair in exasperation. "I'll be back as soon as I can." Looking at Stacy, he said, "We'll check out the car later." He turned and headed toward the back of the house, his long strides making mince-meat of the distance.

Stacy observed the two of them with interest. Mac had towered over the small woman, reminding her of a ha-rassed doberman staring down at a jaunty little para-keet. Maxie wasn't the least bit intimidated. Their conversation, with its blunt acceptance and underlying humor, was definitely not that of a typical boss and hired hand. When Mac disappeared around the corner of the house, Stacy turned to Maxie, blinking at the brilliant rosy fabric. "Great shirt," she said blandly.

Maxie's gaze shifted from Stacy's face to her blouse. After a beat, she said, "I'll take you to my favorite store next time we go into town. You'll like it. Let's get your things out of the car, then you can pick the room you want to stay in."

Shaking her head slowly, Stacy said, "Mac was mis-taken. I'm not staying. If I can just use your phone, I'll call for a tow truck."

Maxie peered into the back window of the red car, then tugged open the door. "Won't do you any good," she said, sticking her head inside the car and looking around. "There was an accident out on the interstate, a big one. I heard about it on the CB. The two tow trucks we have in the area are out there, and they'll be tied up for several hours. By that time it'll be too late for them to start out here. Do you want this bag?"

Stacy automatically held out her hand for the canvas tote bag, while she waited for the other woman to come up for air.

"So Tumbleweed's your handle, huh? From the fuss Long John was making, we kind of expected a kid. 'Course, I don't know what a kid would be doing out here on her own, and I said that very thing to Mac, but did he listen?" Maxie snorted and hauled out a small overnight case and waggled it impatiently behind her until Stacy took it. "'Course he didn't. I could've been a gnat buzzing around his head for all the attention he paid me. What else do you want out of the car? Here, take this." She peered into another canvas bag and held it out.

"I think that's plen—"

"Men don't listen, have you ever noticed? To get their attention you have to whack them alongside the head with something. The heavier the better. Honey, what are you *doing* with all this stuff in the car? It looks like you have everything you own in here. Nobody travels across country hauling a load like this unless they're—"

"Moving," Stacy said, the quiet satisfaction in her voice lost in the other woman's monologue. The plan had been to sashay out of Prudence in a blazing red Corvette, she recalled with a grin, but when she had looked at the growing number of parcels necessary for her "new life," she had known her dream of the slinky car was doomed. At least for the present.

Now, gazing at the four-door Buick, painted a candy apple red, she reminded herself that flexibility was one of the keys to success. That and patience. When she got to Southern California, if she still wanted a Vette, she would get one. But she already suspected that she wouldn't bother. She liked the spacious car. Besides, she was going to a place where individuality, not conformity, was the hallmark. If she wanted to be a free spirit in a red sedan, that's exactly what she would be. She might even have some flowers painted on it.

"There. That should do it." Maxie slammed the back door. "Anything else?"

"Those." Resigned, Stacy pointed at the three books on the front seat. It was only for the night, less than twenty-four hours, she reminded herself bracingly. After all, how much damage could one man who oozed sex from every pore do in that short time?

The answer wasn't long in coming: plenty. She'd be on her way first thing in the morning.

"All of them?" Maxie asked.

Stacy nodded grimly. Planning ahead was another trait she had learned at her daddy's knee, and her daddy had been no slouch when it came to running a business. In fact, any way you looked at him, he had been one smart cookie. So she would take the books and spend the evening reading in her room, and by morning she would be a few chapters closer to understanding life on the cutting edge. And, as a bonus, she would have avoided the one man she had encountered in the last six years who could throw a monkey wrench into her plans.

Knowing precisely what she was doing—heading for the nearest hidey-hole—she wasted no time worrying about discretion and valor. If she chose not to confront temptation in snug jeans, it was her business and hers alone. Watching Maxie haul out the books and push the door closed with a nudge from her hip, she reminded herself that a goal was a goal and hers had been a long time coming. Too long.

Maxie examined the book covers then gazed thoughtfully at Stacy. "*Learning to Meditate, Discovering the Woman Within,* and *Finding Your Personal Power Place?* This is the kind of reading you do on vacation? For fun?" She gave a philosophical shrug. "To each his own, I guess, but I'll take a good romance any day of the week. Here, let me take that case."

She hustled Stacy inside and upstairs, never breaking her running commentary. "I'll show you around later, when you're settled. Mac did all the remodeling. Nice, huh? What do you think of this banister? It's solid oak, and he had the devil's own time getting it in. Here, how about this room?" She opened a door at the end of the hall and looked questioningly at Stacy. "It looks out over the valley, right up to the mountains."

Giving a quick nod, Stacy followed her through the door. Apparently the builder had liked lots of elbow room, Stacy reflected, gazing around the room. In common with the other rooms she had passed through, it had high ceilings, gleaming oak floors and was large enough to hold a square dance. Well, at least one square.

Setting the canvas bag on the floor, she ran her fingers over the peach satin comforter covering the large bed. Even with throw pillows in varying shades of brown and a couple of massive chests, the room remained light and airy.

"Your own bath is behind that door," Maxie said, nodding toward the other end of the room. "All new fixtures, so you don't have to worry about the plumbing. And there's plenty of hot water."

Stacy slowly circled the room, touching the carved drawers on a large bureau and stopping to glance at the spines of the books filling the shelves of an oak case. They ran the gamut of fiction and even included a few old college textbooks. They told her nothing about the personality of the man who owned the house.

"I won't use much water," she said absently, dropping into one of the two flowered, overstuffed chairs that flanked a reading table and lamp. "I'll be leaving in the morning."

"Don't count your chickens, honey."

"What do you mean?" Stacy waited while Maxie plopped down into the chair opposite her.

"I mean if Mac or one of the boys can fix your car, you'll be able to leave tomorrow. Maybe. If they can't, you might be here for several days."

"Several days!"

"Yep." Maxie nodded and held up a finger. "If they have to send for a tow truck, your car gets hauled away." A second finger joined the first. "Then Joe or Pete—the only two guys within fifty miles with a truck—have to figure out what's wrong with it. If they do and have the stuff to fix it, you're outta here in a couple of days. If they have to order a part—" two more fingers and a thumb lifted "—your guess is as good as mine. Five days, six, maybe a week."

"I can't stay here a week!" Stacy said in dismay.

Maxie's white brows rose. "Why? You in a hurry to get somewhere?"

"Well . . . no." Stacy shook her head slowly. "It's just that . . . you don't even know me." And she didn't want to be exposed to Mac McClain's brand of savagely restrained sensuality a minute longer than she had to be. She gazed at the older woman, gloomily aware that her expressive face undoubtedly mirrored her dismay. She had learned a lot in the last six years, but apparently one thing would never change. She would never have a poker face.

"I know," Stacy said, brightening. "If we do have to get a tow truck, I'll just go with them and stay in a motel."

"What motel?" Maxi asked dryly. "Pete and Joe have gas stations. Out in the middle of nowhere. They each have a small house filled with a wife and kids."

"No motel?" Stacy asked in disbelief.

"No motel."

Thirty minutes later Stacy sat alone in the kitchen drinking a glass of lemonade and waiting for Maxie to return. Part of her mind was occupied with what she had seen on Maxie's whirlwind tour of the house. It was a warm and welcoming home, perfect for a large, boisterous family. Mac was a magnificent craftsman, retaining the old-fashioned charm of the house as he upgraded and modernized. She pictured him working on the beautiful oak cabinets and doors, and knew that his big, lean hands were capable of coaxing whatever he wanted from the raw wood. She had a sinking feeling that they could do exactly the same with a woman.

"California."

She murmured the word aloud, said it again, using it as a mantra. For four long years she had dreamed of freedom, of life in a place at the opposite end of the spectrum from Prudence, Kansas. Not that there was anything intrinsically wrong with Prudence, she allowed. In fact, as small towns went, it was a very nice one, with good, solid, dependable people. The problem—if there was one—was with her, not Prudence.

She couldn't remember exactly when she'd begun yearning for more distant horizons, but it had been somewhere in her teens. She pored over college catalogs from both coasts and all points in between, dreaming dreams and knowing that somewhere, in a new world, adventure awaited her. Her mother's death changed her plans, though. She attended a local college to remain near her father. Later, when she was finishing her M.B.A., she allowed herself to dream again, of distant places and a life-style where she mingled with unconventional and amusing, eccentric people. Yes, adventure was definitely on her mind. But once again her plans had been changed. That had been four years ago when her father had died.

She had stepped into his shoes and run the family business, dealing with the small-town businessmen who wouldn't take a "whippersnapper" of a girl seriously. The only way she knew how was by becoming Ms. Sullivan, a brisk, efficient, suitably attired executive. And knowing that the local grapevine was always up and running, she stopped potential trouble and gossip by putting her social life on permanent hold.

It hadn't been easy, but if she had to do it all over again, she would make the same decisions. Her aunts and uncles had their savings invested in the business, and the company employed many of the people in town. So whatever she had sacrificed in order to be taken seriously as the major business owner in town, had been worth it. But this time she had made it. She was on her way and she wouldn't slow down until she reached the Pacific Ocean. This time nothing—and no one—would stop her.

The slam of the screen door brought her back to the present, and the sound of boot heels on the floor as well as a trill of nerves told her who was negligently leaning against the door frame.

"Where's Maxie?" Mac asked.

"She took a box of food over to the bunkhouse." Stacy tightened her hands around the perspiring glass and turned to face him. One quick glance assured her that her imagination hadn't been working overtime. No kind fate had turned him into a lovable teddy bear. He was still too big, too taut and too focused.

On her.

Lethal. The word had occurred to her more than once in the past several hours, beginning when he'd hustled her into the pickup and climbed in beside her. She had felt crowded, even though there was ample room between them. The impression had not dissipated, even when he'd withdrawn into himself and done an imitation of an iceman. Especially not then. He hadn't taken his eyes off the road, hadn't made a gesture that a sensible woman would find threatening. But she hadn't felt sensible. Or reasonable. She had felt like a big cat was stalking her.

Stacy blinked at the thought. It wasn't a comforting one. Life in Prudence hadn't equipped her to deal with stalking cats.

"I thought the men ate here, in the house," she said hastily to break the charged silence.

"They do." Mac pulled out the chair next to hers, angling it so it faced her before he sat down. "But there's a kitchen in the bunkhouse, and we keep it stocked so they don't have to bother Maxie if they get hungry in between meals. How's your room?"

"Fine. Very comfortable."

"Good. Looks like you'll be using it for a while," he said blandly.

Stacy carefully set her glass on the table. "My car?" she asked with deep foreboding.

He grinned, shaking his head. "Sweetheart, the buzzards are circling over it."

"But it's brand-new!"

Mac nodded. "That's the problem. If it was old, we could probably patch it up. We keep some of ours going with spit and rubber bands. But with all the electronic bells and whistles they're putting in new cars, we don't have a clue. It's probably a circuit board."

Stacy sighed. "And what does that mean?"

"A tow truck. Tomorrow at the earliest. And unless you're real lucky, parts ordered from the nearest dealer who may or may not have to order them from a distributor."

"But that could take days!"

"Yep."

Stacy threw him an annoyed look. Mac was leaning back in his chair, balancing on the rear legs, his expression as bland as his voice. She resisted the temptation to give him a nudge. The way her luck was running, he'd probably just leap to his feet like the big cat he reminded her of and then there'd be hell to pay. She blinked at the thought of his big body exploding into action and knew she didn't want to be the catalyst that set him off. What was more, she didn't want to be anywhere around when it happened.

She managed not to sigh again. At least not audibly. "In that case, could one of your men take me into the nearest town?"

His black brows rose in questioning arcs. "Are we talking emergency here?"

Annoyed, Stacy closed her eyes. Years earlier, her Uncle Evert had told her she couldn't lie worth spit. She wasn't much better at it now than she had been then. "No," she said bluntly, glaring at him. "No emergency. It's just a matter of... convenience."

"Yours or mine?"

Stacy wanted to shriek in exasperation at the mild question. She took a determined breath, reminding herself that she had worked long and hard to control her hair-trigger temper. No one, not one single person in the last several years had succeeded in making her lose it. Not one solitary soul had wiped out years of discipline, had made her want to reach out for the nearest object and throw it.

Until now.

"Your convenience," she said as convincingly as possible, clasping her hands tightly around the glass of lemonade. After all, it really was. It was one thing for him to take in an unexpected guest for one night, another thing entirely to be stuck with said guest for a week or more.

"If that's the case," Mac said calmly, "no."

"No?" Stacy stared at him. *"No?"*

He shook his head. "No. It's more convenient for me to keep my men on the job than to lose a day's work driving you all over the country."

"Mac, I don't think you've thought this through," she said in a determinedly practical voice. "You're talking about having a stranger in your house for seven or eight days."

"Fifteen rooms," he reminded her.

"People need a certain amount of privacy," she said urgently.

"Big rooms," he added in a lazy voice.

"You shouldn't have to be concerned about people intruding when you're in your own house."

"If it'll make you feel better, I'll put a sign on any door I don't want you to open."

"That's not the point!" ·

"What is the point? You want to be entertained every minute of the day?"

"Of course not," she said, stung. "I'm quite capable of taking care of myself."

Mac shrugged. "Then I don't see the problem."

Stubborn, she decided grimly. The man was mule stubborn. And thick. Subtleties were wasted on him. In the midst of her peeved reflections, she realized he had asked her a question. She shifted her gaze from the open neck of his shirt to his face. "What?"

"I asked if we've settled everything. If we have, I'll see you at dinner."

"No," she said slowly, knowing instinctively that he wouldn't like what she was going to say. "We haven't. Not quite everything. I would pay my way at a motel, and I plan to do the same here. I'll expect a bill when I leave."

She was right.

He didn't like it. Not a bit.

Mac's chair thumped down on all four legs. Temper coiled in his black eyes and for a split second blazed out at her. "You'll wait until hell freezes over, lady. Nobody pays for my hospitality. Nobody!"

After the way Mac had stalked out earlier, slamming the door behind him and leaving her to deal with her own temper and guilt, the noise and confusion of dinner was a welcome relief.

Ten men streamed through the door, all in pointed boots and bearing names like Slim, Red, Curly and Doc. There was no apparent connection between the names and the men, at least not as far as Stacy could tell. Slim was chunky and just slightly taller than Stacy, Red was tall with grizzled gray hair, Curly was the bald foreman and Doc wasn't a doctor.

"Too bad about your car," Curly said to her once the platters of fried chicken and mounds of mashed potatoes and gravy had disappeared. "Several of us are pretty fair mechanics, but when we poked around we couldn't even make her cough."

Stacy carefully avoided looking at Mac. When he had introduced her to the men, he had still been simmering with anger. "I really appreciate your help," she said with a smile that touched everywhere except the head of the table. "I hope it didn't take you away from your work for too long."

"Aw, hell, Stacy," Slim began, then broke off when the others turned to glare at him. He cleared his throat. "Uh, heck, Stacy, it gave us an excuse to get out of the sun for a while. Anyway, we didn't do anything."

"You tried," she said firmly, giving him another smile that made him blink. "That's what counts."

"Is this going to be a problem for you?" Red asked.

Stacy turned to him. "Problem?"

"I mean, do you have to be somewhere at a set time, will anyone be worried about you?"

Their curiosity and interest were palpable. Since she refused to look at Mac, she had no idea if his face reflected the same undivided attention. "I'm on a ... driving vacation," she said finally. "I have no set schedule, and I'm just seeing parts of the country I've never visited before. When I'm done, I'll end up in California."

"Why there?"

"To live?"

"To work?"

"You have a job there?"

"Is that where your family is?"

Stacy leaned back in her chair as the questions flew at her from all directions. Privacy was obviously a concept that had little meaning here, she decided with a flicker of amusement, wondering what had happened to the old Western practice of not asking personal questions. Here, anything and everything seemed to be for public consumption. Her amusement faded as she looked around the table. As different as the men were, they were strong and competent, in touch with the basic things of life.

She thought of the books in her room and closed her eyes with a quiet sigh. Opening them, she made a rapid decision. Some things *were* private, and she was neither going to explain her present life-style or rationalize. Especially not to this pragamatic, well-grounded bunch. They wouldn't understand. Looking for adventure, with a capital *A*, wouldn't sound nearly as exciting to them as it did to someone who had lived in Prudence for most of her twenty-eight years.

"Nope," she said cheerfully, "no family in California." No friends, either, but they didn't have to know that. "Eventually I'll get a job there, but for now, I'm fancy-free. So to answer your question, it's inconvenient to have the car break down, but not really a problem. The only awkward part is knowing that you're stuck with me until it's done."

She darted a sideways glance at Mac and almost choked. His level gaze was pinned on her, watching every move she made. Temper, coiled and hot, still gleamed in his dark eyes. She'd have to do something about that, she thought with another sigh. Soon.

The men began drifting away, and when just the two of them were left at the table, Stacy cleared her throat. "Mac?"

His brows rose in a silent question.

He wasn't going to make it easy. Of course, there was no reason why he should, she thought, remembering her parting shot. Her *petty* parting shot.

"I want to apologize," she said quietly, her green eyes meeting his dark ones. "I was rude. I've never been in the position of accepting such sweeping hospitality before, and I've just learned that I'm much better at giving than receiving. Will you forgive me?''

He stood up and held out his hand to her. When she touched it, his fingers closed around hers and he tugged her to her feet. ''Forgiven,'' he said in a voice that still held a remnant of anger. ''But, Stacy.'' He stopped herding her toward the door and waited until she looked up at him. ''Don't try anything like that again, or we both might end up regretting it.''

When her eyes widened, he nodded and said evenly, ''Now, do you want to see the outside of this place or not?''

Three

Stacy slitted one eye open and looked around. She was sitting cross-legged in the shade of a towering ponderosa pine with her hands resting on her knees, palms up. By now, she had breathed deeply, counted backward from ten three different times and was supposed to be centered. According to chapter two, being centered meant, among other things, being mentally concentrated, bodily relaxed and emotionally calm.

She had a sneaking suspicion that it didn't mean worrying about pinecones falling on her head or scooting around like a crab because the long, brittle needles from the tree were poking into her bottom.

There was definitely more to the process than the encouraging tone of the first chapter had led her to believe. In fact, she had decided that the book had a serious flaw. It said nothing at all about dealing with a mind that refused to settle down and attend to business, a mind that skittered and jumped around like a flea on a long-haired dog. The book assumed that the reader was disciplined.

It was wrong.

Stacy opened her other eye, contemplating an ant crawling up her bare leg. The ant was as distracted as she was, she thought, watching it busily circle her kneecap, hustle back down toward her ankle then make a sharp right to investigate her calf. But that was apparently an ant's way of life, it spent all its time dodging and darting. Her restiveness was temporary, she assured herself—induced by the changing expressions in Mac's dark eyes.

Stacy sighed and slumped against the rough tree trunk. She had been on the ranch for less than twenty-four hours, and he was already making her crazy. The trouble was, she couldn't read the blasted man. She didn't know what he wanted, and that bothered her. A lot. Because another one of her daddy's truisms was, find out what a man wants and you've got a bead on him. It had worked for her all of her adult life. Worked very well.

Until now.

Mac simply didn't fit into any of the neat little slots. Of course, one aspect wasn't a mystery at all. He was a rancher from the tip of his wide-brimmed hat to the soles of his leather boots. He had lots of acres and lots of horses and knew exactly what to do with both of them. He wanted to be left alone by people, the government and the IRS, to do what he did best: run a ranch. It was the other part that had her baffled, the indefinable aura that declared a man interested in a woman or not interested.

On the surface it often seemed that he wasn't—and that was fine with her, she reflected, shifting restlessly. Just fine.

Absolutely and unequivocally fine.

Last night, on the fifty-cent tour, he had been ... courteous. He had taken her through the barn, the garage that housed a variety of trucks and cars and around the outside of the house, politely answering her questions. It would have been reassuring if her instincts hadn't been clamoring, keeping her on edge.

For one thing he had still been a bit stiff about her demand to pay him, and she wasn't sure what form his anger would take. On top of that, he did want her. He didn't say it and he didn't show it, but it couldn't have been more obvious if the statement had been stamped in red ink on his forehead.

But that wasn't the kind of wanting her father had discussed with her. What did Mac want *from* her? That was the real question. A quick, one-night stand? She shook her head. In this day and age that was not only stupid, it verged on suicidal. So what then? An affair for the time that she'd be here? That wasn't much better.

Stacy straightened her legs, staring down at her crossed ankles thoughtfully. It couldn't be much else. She had no illusions about her appearance. She wasn't the kind of woman who drove men mad with passion. Granted, what with her jazzy new haircut and clothes, she had improved in the last few weeks, but she had been looking in her mirror long enough to know what Mac saw when he glanced at her. The basics hadn't changed that much—intelligent eyes that had a tendency these days to sparkle with enthusiasm, a nose that was neither too large nor too small and a body that was about the same. All in all, there was nothing to make a man act like a predator about to pounce. And that's what he seemed like at times—just often enough to keep her instincts twitching.

Stacy leaned forward, lured the energetic ant on to her finger and gently deposited it on the needle-strewn ground. Watching it bustle away, she gave a gusty sigh, knowing her instincts were right. She may have lived in a backwater town most of her life, but she hadn't been in a convent, and every now and then she *knew* that Mac was a hungry, stalking man—whether he showed it or not.

The air around them had been thick with tension last night. She had felt it in her blood and bones. But while it had tightened her voice and dried her throat, he had casually discussed his horses. They were Arabians, he'd told her, graceful animals built for speed and endurance.

It was both annoying and disconcerting because it made her wonder if she was imagining the whole thing. Wonder if she saw hunger burning in his eyes because she was a frustrated woman approaching the big three-oh. A woman who had lived alone for too long.

Stacy's head snapped up when a hat plopped on her knee. "Mac! You scared me to death! What are you doing creeping around here like an Indian?"

Mac dropped down beside her, propping his lean length on his forearm. "You were so deep in thought, you wouldn't have heard me if I'd been a bear."

"Bear! Good Lord, don't tell me you've got them, too." Stacy jerked upright, throwing an uneasy glance over her shoulder.

"Relax." Mac cupped her shoulder with his long fingers, keeping them there until she sagged back against the tree. "We have some, but they're up there," he nodded at the distant, jagged peaks. "They don't come down this far very often. Even if they did, they'd be more scared of you than you are of them."

"Don't count on it." She eyed him doubtfully, then tapped her finger on the brim of the straw hat resting on her knee. "What's this?"

"A little something that people up here wear so the sun doesn't fry their brains. You'll put it on whenever you leave the house."

Stacy eyed him from beneath raised brows, annoyed as much at the direct order as the tone in which it was delivered. "I will?" she asked pleasantly.

"You will." His voice was uncompromising. "Anytime you walk out the door between sunup and dusk."

"I'm used to the sun," she protested. "Kansas isn't exactly a rain forest, you know. I never wear a hat."

Mac wasn't impressed. "You do now," he said flatly. "Until you leave." He studied her mutinous expression and added in a soft, level voice, "Don't push me on this one, honey."

Stacy dug her back into the tree and narrowed her eyes. "In my neck of the woods, that would be considered a threat."

He shook his head and with an effortless movement surged to his feet. "Nope. I don't waste time making threats. That was a promise. Now I want yours."

"My what?"

"Promise. That you'll wear it."

He waited, his hands resting loosely on his hips, deliberately towering over her. Since she was going to have the run of the ranch for the next few days, and since— whether she knew it or not—she already had the hands so firmly wrapped around her little finger that they wouldn't argue with her, this was one battle he was going to win. Right here, right now. Visitors to the desert expected the heat and prepared for it, but in the mountains, lulled by the cooler air, they either forgot or flat out didn't know that the sun was just as potent. They learned the hard way.

So he stood and waited, knowing he couldn't back down an inch, wondering what was going on behind those gorgeous green eyes. She looked like an infuriated cat, ready to leap, claw and spit, but he had a hunch that she wouldn't. Beneath all that enthusiasm and her lunatic habit of dropping on the nearest flat surface to meditate whenever the mood struck her, she had a surprising air of control about her. Just the same, he was glad she didn't have a two-by-four within reach of her tightly laced fingers.

The silence stretched out, reminding him that dealing with women was always risky. He never knew what the hell they were thinking. They had a way of looking small and fragile then confounding you with the strength of an Amazon. But one thing you could always count on: they were as obstinate and contrary as a barn full of mules.

He had learned to pick his fights with them carefully. He had also learned that the quickest way to get his point across was sheer intimidation. So now, using his height and silence, he waited.

"All right," she said in a goaded voice. "I'll wear the blasted hat."

Silently he bent over, plucked the hat off her knee and dropped it on her head. He wrapped his fingers around her wrist and pulled her to her feet. "Do you ride?"

Stacy tugged her hand from his and brushed off the seat of her shorts. When she finished, she asked cautiously, "Ride what?"

Mac stared at her. She wasn't joking. "Honey, you're on a ranch. In Arizona. What do you think I'm talking about, an ostrich? A horse! Do you ride a horse?"

Stacy shook her head. Emphatically. "No. I don't. And it's not on my list, so don't even think about it."

"What list?"

"The list of things I'm going to do." She tilted back her head and peered at him beneath the brim of her hat. "Trust me on this, Mac. Riding something that's bigger than me, weighs about a ton and is afraid of a squawking bird is definitely not on my list."

He grinned. He couldn't help himself. She was so damned cute. "You're kidding. Right?"

She shook her head again. "Wrong. If my two legs or my four wheels can't get me there, I don't go."

"Look, honey," he soothed, "I have this little mare that would be perfect for you. The one I showed you last night."

"The one that spit on me?"

He sighed sharply. "Stacy, horses don't spit."

"Oh, really? Then what was that stuff I had to scrape off my shirt?"

He ignored that bit of humor. At least, he supposed she was being funny. "I thought I could take you around the ranch this afternoon."

"You did that," she reminded him. "Last night."

He stared down at her. She was serious. "Stacy, that was the yard."

"Oh." She stared thoughtfully at the third button on his shirt. It was open, and she could see a tangle of dark hair on his chest. She wanted to touch it, she realized with a sense of shock. To run her finger down the center of that wedge and see if the hair was as crisp and soft as it looked.

And that had to be one of the dumbest ideas she'd had in a long time. It ranked right along with playing with a stick of lighted dynamite.

"In that case, I'd love to see the rest of the place," she said politely, lying through her teeth. "As long as we do it in a truck. But how about this evening? I promised Maxie I'd help her with dinner."

"Okay. Later." Mac nodded abruptly and turned away.

It was wrong, all wrong, she thought, watching him walk in the direction of the barn. It didn't matter how they went, truck, Jeep, wagon or pogo stick, she shouldn't be alone with him. He was dangerous. And she was vulnerable. Looking at him, Stacy realized with a sense of real shock, exactly how vulnerable she was.

Four years, she thought numbly. Four years without a man in her life. Dates, yes. To civic functions and church affairs. Tepid evenings with pleasant men. None that would interest the wagging tongues in Prudence, that would mark her as frivolous or threaten her status as a responsible businesswoman. None with a man who looked at her with hot eyes, who touched her with hands both hard and gentle. There were no men in those four years who had made her heart pound and her blood roar through her veins like a freight train. None who had made her feel hot and panicky when he got too close.

None like Mac.

Would she have felt so defenseless with any man? she wondered, recalling the sand-colored shirt straining across his muscular chest. If any other cowboy, equally tall, lean, broad shouldered and fiercely masculine had appeared on the scene, would it have been the same?

Or was it just Mac?

Stacy gave a small shrug, reminding herself that it didn't matter. As her father had often reminded her, you play the cards that you're dealt, and apparently, Mac was her next hand.

Sometimes, life was really rotten.

Why couldn't a nice, roly-poly grandfather have rescued her? Or a teenager with acne and no older male relatives? Or any man with a few less hormones raging through his body? She would at least have had a bit of practice before she hit the big time with someone like Mac.

Problems. She was tired of dealing with them as character-building assets, Stacy thought moodily. She had racked up enough character for three lifetimes. She mentally added another section to her growing list: she would learn to handle problems in a more positive manner, preferably by walking away from them or letting someone else cope with them. And she would begin as soon as she figured out what to do about sharing a house with Mac for seven days.

It didn't matter that the wonderful old house had fifteen rooms, it was still too small. It didn't matter that there were ten cowboys and the formidable Maxie around, he still crowded her.

Why me? she wondered morosely. All she wanted was a nice, easy, meandering trip to California. And adventure. Something to add color and pizzazz to her life without complicating it. Was that too much to ask?

Remembering the lazy interest in Mac's eyes, she reflected that it probably was.

Then again, she thought with the honesty that had become second nature, she could be imagining the whole thing. Maybe Mac *was* just being a polite host, maybe he really didn't look at her as if she were fascinating and . . . tasty. God only knew she didn't have enough experience to know for certain. There was every chance in the world that she was overreacting. It could be that after her sterile existence in Prudence, she was just a tad off balance.

And hopeful.

Stacy was still brooding over that grim possibility several hours later when they all gathered for dinner around the large table. As usual, conversation didn't begin until most of the food was gone.

"Boss, when you going to show Stacy the rest of the place?" Curly asked thickly, swallowing a mouthful of Maxie's cherry pie.

Red smiled at Stacy. "Just tell me when, and I'll saddle the horses."

"Stacy doesn't ride."

Mac's quiet statement couldn't have had more effect if he had shouted it through a bullhorn, Stacy decided, picking at the cherries on her plate with stoic determination. "Great pie, Maxie," she said finally, breaking the stunned silence. She glanced around at ten staring men, mildly annoyed. What was the big deal, anyway? A lot of people in the world didn't ride horses.

Maxie looked at the staring men disgustedly. "You have to understand, Stacy, these are men who would ride from the barn to the kitchen if I'd let them tie up horses outside the door."

"You don't ride?" Red and Doc asked at the same time.

"Ever?" Slim washed down his pie with a slug of coffee.

"Never." Stacy shook her head, grinning at the ten faces all bearing the same expression of consternation. "Come on, guys, give me a break here. I grew up with skates and bikes. Then cars. I was in Kansas, remember? In a small town, with no ranges to ride. Besides, Prudence is so small that we walked most of the time.''

They looked at her pityingly.

Stacy sighed. ''Look, it's okay. Really. I don't feel deprived. I never felt deprived. In fact—''

''I'll teach you how to ride.'' The offer came from three directions at once.

''Heck,'' Slim drawled, ''it's as easy as—''

''Falling off a horse?'' Stacy grinned, shaking her head. ''Thanks, guys, I appreciate the offers. But no thanks.''

''But—''

''Anyone for more pie?'' Maxie said hastily. With all the subtlety of a smoldering branding iron, she turned to Stacy and changed the subject. ''Why don't you tell us about Prudence, what you did there and all.''

This time, while Stacy silently did a rapid editing of her recent history, eleven men waited. Mac's black eyes never left her face. Stacy hesitated, knowing how it was to live in a small town or an out-of-the-way place. New faces were welcome at the dinner table, and their stories were rehashed long after they had traveled on. That was all well and good, and she was willing to provide what entertainment she could, but the last thing she wanted to talk about was life in Prudence. At least, not as it really was. It was too depressing. And now that she had left it behind, she wanted to forget the responsible and tedious Ms. Sullivan of SullCo, Inc.

She had had more fun in the past two weeks than she'd had in all of the last six years combined, she realized with a small sense of shock. She liked the new Stacy Sullivan she had created, and she was just vain enough to want her new image to be the one remembered. When she left Mac's ranch, she'd rather have the men talking about Tumbleweed the drifter than the drudge.

A quick glance at Mac assured her that his dark gaze hadn't left her face. Her expressive face. Sighing, she acknowledged that the trick would be to leave that impression without telling an outright lie.

Of course, she reflected, omitting dull facts wasn't precisely lying. It was called poetic license. All storytellers worth their salt did it. And she *did* have the list, she reminded herself. That was part of her new life. So if she wanted to leave them with the image of a free spirit who sat on flat rocks to meditate, she was entitled, wasn't she?

She was.

"Prudence is small, with less than five thousand people," she said slowly. "The main business in town is a company that makes labels."

"Labels?" Red looked puzzled.

Stacy nodded. "You know, the kind you put on file folders, and the little round colored suckers that you slap on everything. A lot of them that you see in stores were made in Prudence."

"You work there?" Curly asked.

"Yep." She nodded again. "Along with almost everyone else in town. I was born and raised in Prudence. My first and last job was at the factory."

Red pushed his pie plate away and plunked his elbows on the table. "So what are you doing driving around the country?"

"Ah." She grinned. "That's the good part. I, uh, inherited some money," she explained rapidly. "From my grandmother," she added, blithely eliminating the woman who had been at rest beneath a granite headstone for over twenty-five years.

Slim smiled. "So you quit your job?"

"In a blaze of glory," she agreed, her eyes sparkling. "I sold my house, had the biggest garage sale the town has ever had and left." The sale would have been a lot bigger if it hadn't been for all the aunts and uncles, she recalled. When they heard of her plans, they had plunked themselves down in her living room and reminded her how fond they were of various items in the house. The day before the sale, a moving truck had delivered most of her furniture to their already overcrowded homes.

"You sold everything?" Maxie demanded, looking scandalized.

"Everything," Stacy agreed complacently. "All I have left is what's in the car."

Curly cleared his throat. "Is it true what Long John said? That you don't have any family?"

Stacy shook her head and held up four fingers. "Nope. Two aunts, two uncles. They're all pets, and I love them dearly."

"Didn't they—"

"Mind me leaving?" She nodded. "Yes, they did, but they invited the whole town to a party for me and sent me on my way with their blessings."

"Why?"

The blunt question came from Mac.

"Why? Because they love me," she said softly. And because they knew she had given too many years to duty and responsibility, partly for their benefit.

"So what will you do now?"

She shrugged her slim shoulders. "Wait for my car to be fixed."

"Then what?"

"Travel." She brightened at the thought. "Take off in any direction I want, stop when and where I want, stay as long as I want."

"And end up in California."

"Eventually."

"And what do you expect to find there?"

"Adventure." Her green eyes sparkled. "Different people—"

"You got that right," Mac muttered.

"Exciting places, new ideas."

Mac's assessing gaze took in her barely suppressed excitement. She couldn't wait to go galloping off in a new direction, he thought grimly. The first chance she got, she'd bundle all that energy and vitality into the bright red car and shoot down the road without a backward glance.

That was fine with him.

The hell it was.

But it should be. She had been on the ranch a little over twenty-four hours, and he was already acting like a stallion catching scent of a mare in heat. On the plus side, he had managed to keep his hands off her.

So far.

It hadn't been easy and it wasn't getting any easier. His stomach muscles knotted when she looked at Curly, her face alight with amusement. He didn't need this kind of aggravation, he reminded himself. His life was organized, right on schedule, all according to his long-term plans. The house was almost done, just needing a bit of fine-tuning and furniture, also on schedule. The final details were waiting until he brought home a woman. The woman. His wife, the mother of his future children.

She would be a strong, vital woman, he reminded himself. One who would help him carry on the McClain name in the hard country where McClains had lived for five generations. She wouldn't be a pretty painted butterfly, a hummingbird, hovering one second and gone the next. She wouldn't—

A soft gurgle of laughter stopped him dead in his tracks. The sound made him think of moonlight, rumpled sheets and long, sleek legs. Of his room, his bed and Stacy, her glossy brown hair sliding like silk over his chest. It made him wonder if she would come to a man with the same joyous enthusiasm and vitality.

His whole body tightened at the thought, and he knew he was going to find out.

Four

"So, tell me," Mac said, shooting the battered pickup over the ruts in the winding dirt road. "Exactly what kind of adventure are you looking for?"

"Mac, for heaven's sake, what's the big rush?" Stacy demanded with a harassed look, bracing herself as the truck bounced and lunged up a moderate grade. She deliberately ignored the question. It seemed to her that she had answered enough of them at the dinner table. Turning sideways to face him, she leaned back against the locked door so she could scowl at him in comfort. "I was going to help Maxie with the dishes."

"She doesn't like people cluttering up the kitchen."

"Right," she agreed dryly. "I suppose that's why she let me peel a ton of potatoes this afternoon." Her frown deepened as she gazed at his profile. An arrogant profile, she decided. Well, that was fitting, he was an arrogant man.

He hadn't asked her to come, she fumed, switching her gaze to his hands. He had simply stopped her when she reached for a stack of plates on the table. Stopped her by lazily getting to his feet, wrapping his lean fingers around her wrist and tugging her close to his side. When he'd released her, he'd dropped his arm over her shoulders before she could move, the sheer weight of it keeping her plastered against him, and led her out the front door.

"Do you always steamroll over people like this?" she asked with genuine curiosity. "Hasn't anyone ever told you about saying a simple please when you want something? It does work, you know."

"Not if you're dealing with someone who's as stubborn as she is contrary. Adventure," he prompted, with a lazy grin. "What kind?"

Stacy shrugged, giving up, at least for the moment. "Whatever's out there," she replied honestly.

"Out where?"

She waved a hand, encompassing the green valley, the mountains and everything that lay beyond them. "There. Everywhere." She shrugged. "Anywhere. New places, new faces."

"And you think you'll find something you didn't have in Patience?"

Stacy eyed him with annoyance. "Don't hold back, Mac," she said dryly. "If you want to know something, feel free to ask. And it's Prudence."

"Right." One side of his mouth turned up in amusement. "So, do you?"

She closed her eyes briefly in exasperation. "Think I'll find something different? I know I will."

"How?"

"How could I not? Mac, I told you, my hometown is *small*. There's one movie that can't be dignified by calling it a theater, a bowling alley, a street full of bars and another street full of churches. *Anything's* more exciting than that."

"So you're on your way to bigger and better things?"

"Absolutely." She nodded, pleased that he was finally beginning to understand. But she didn't want him too understanding, she realized with a start, remembering The Image. She was Tumbleweed, footloose and without a care in the world, not an escapee from a humdrum existence in Smalltown, U.S.A.

Wondering if she had already given more away than she'd planned, she added brightly, "Of course, I was always trying something new and different, flitting from job to job in the factory." Well, that was partially true—if dreams counted. And she *had* started in the mail room and, at one time or another, worked almost every station in the company.

"If you hated it that much, why did you stay so long?"

"I didn't hate it," she answered slowly, knowing it was the truth. "I just got tired of doing the same thing, being in the same place. As it was, I took off the first chance I got."

"Sounds to me like you have a low threshold of boredom."

She nodded vigorously. "You're absolutely right. That's why I'm on an open-ended schedule, traveling down new roads."

He took his eyes off the dusty road and studied her thoughtfully. "Did you go to college?"

"Yep. The whole works, lived on campus and all."

"And?"

She shrugged. The Image, she reminded herself. "I dabbled in art, tried a pottery class, gave creative writing a whirl." She thought a moment before adding, "I also took karate and was on the swim team." It was all the truth. As far as it went. In all honesty, though—depressing as it was—she had only truly excelled in her business classes.

She thought she saw a glimmer of disapproval in Mac's eyes and wasn't surprised. Maxie liked to talk, and from everything she had said, Stacy had gathered that Mac was a man who cherished ties. A traditional man. He believed in family, hard work and responsibility. He would neither understand nor approve of her leaving her aunts and uncles and hightailing it out of Prudence. He had more than a touch of the life-is-real-life-is-earnest quality about him, she reflected, and she had a strong feeling that he was considering the option of giving her a good shaking and following it up with a lecture about doing one's duty. Her lips twitched at the thought.

"So you've spent your life, as much as circumstances allowed, doing exactly what you wanted to do?"

Stacy smiled. "Sounds heavenly, doesn't it?" she asked blandly. "Ever tried it?"

"Every now and then." He gave a shrug of his massive shoulders. "It's not all it's cut out to be. How many men did you run through while you were experimenting?"

"I beg your pardon?"

Mac would have had to be deaf or extremely stupid not to hear the warning in her frosty voice. Since she was confident that he was neither, she decided that it was just another example of the cowboy's misguided belief that the male of the species was a superior being whose chore

in life was to take care of the little woman. In all ways.
Even if the little woman wasn't his. And even if it meant
that he was being insulting, arrogant and completely out
of line.

"I said—"

"Never mind," she interrupted hastily, glaring at him.
"I heard you the first time. I just couldn't believe that
you were being so—"

"Male?"

His quick glance was as infuriating as it was disturb-
ing. The last thing she wanted was to have Mac making
macho noises, getting possessive, she assured herself.
She was in no mood to deal with the idiocy of male ter-
ritorial instincts.

"No, rude," she said coolly.

With an impatient twist of the steering wheel, Mac
pulled off the road and slid to a stop. They had been
climbing steadily for some time and had reached the tree
line minutes earlier. The heavy branches from a tangled
growth of piñons threw shade over the truck.

Mac killed the motor and turned sideways to gaze at
her, resting his arm on the back of the seat. "You're ag-
gravating enough to make a man more than rude," he
said finally.

"*I* am!" Stacy repeated, outraged. "You're saying it's
my fault? Well if that doesn't beat the spots off a pig. All
I was doing was answering your questions. And if you
had the courtesy of a flea, you wouldn't have asked them
in the first place. You're supposed to wait for people to
offer information about themselves, not grill them as if
they were . . . suspects or something," she said lamely.

It was hard to stay angry with Mac looking at her the
way he was, she thought, scooting back against the door
until the handle gouged her spine. Nervously, she

brought her knees close to her chest and looped her arms around them. She absently acknowledged the defensiveness of the position, deciding that it was justified. She *felt* defensive. Mac was staring at her and he had the look of a starving man staring at a table loaded with his favorite foods.

"Yeah, I'd say it's your fault." His cool tone matched hers. "You might have convinced the truckers that you're everybody's kid sister, and you might have my men eating out of that soft little palm of yours, but I'll tell you something, lady. I'm not buying it."

"You're not?" She didn't have the foggiest idea what he was talking about.

He shook his head. "We both know that you pack a kick like a Missouri mule."

Stacy's eyes widened. "We do?"

"And I'll be damned if I'm going to treat you like somebody's kid sister."

"You're not?" She cleared her dry throat, wondering what was coming next. She could hardly wait. Never, ever, had she had a conversation with a man that was so bewildering and so utterly fascinating.

"Damned straight I'm not," he said aggressively. "And don't bother asking why. That's another thing we both know. Because you are one hell of a sexy lady."

"*I* am?" Stacy blinked at him, stunned. "I mean, I *am?*"

"You are." Sudden amusement gleamed in his eyes. "Beat the spots off a pig?"

Stacy flushed. "It's something my uncle says." Her eyes narrowed, irritation replacing her momentary chagrin, even overriding her fascination. "And don't change the subject. You were being rude and overbearing." She waited, then prompted, "A gentleman would apologize."

Mac eyed her thoughtfully. "You're right. I shouldn't have asked you about your past."

"I accept your apology," she said promptly. "Belated and obscure as it is."

"Because what I really want to know is if there's a man in your life right now."

"What?"

He leaned closer and ran a finger across her bare left hand. "Looks like there's no husband. Is there a lover?"

Wrath gathered in her green eyes. "I don't believe this! Even you aren't this thickheaded. What on earth gives you the right to ask me a question like that?"

"Because I intend to be the next man in your life."

She stared at him, speechless. When she finally gathered her wits, she shook her head, holding out her hand, palm toward him, like a cop stopping traffic. "Oh, no. No. Wrong. I'm only going to be here for a week. Less, if I'm lucky. You are definitely not on my list."

"Write me in."

The three words were slow and sexy and raised the temperature in the truck about fifteen degrees.

Still shaking her head, Stacy slid her free hand to the door behind her, clasping the metal handle jutting into her back. She pushed down, knowing that even if she had to fall out headfirst, she'd do it. She'd do whatever it took to get away, because for the first time in her life, she was caught in the spell of a man's words, by the tension behind them, by the look in his eyes and the touch of his hand. For the first time she felt an overwhelming need for a man, to touch him, and it scared the living daylights out of her.

What made Mac so dangerous, she realized with a sense of shock, was the fact that he believed every word he said. By some cosmic fluke, she had driven halfway across the country to meet a man on a deserted road who thought she was the sexiest thing that had ever walked down the pike.

And he wasn't a bit shy about saying so.

What made the situation even more volatile was the fact that she felt exactly the same way about him. And while it went against the grain to be practical about it, somebody had to be, dammit! One of them had to keep in mind that she was just traveling through, and he was a man whose roots ran deep. One of them had to think beyond this very moment.

"You can't get out that way," Mac said calmly, cupping one of her knees with his large, callused hand. His eyes narrowed when she shivered. "The handle's broken. I have to open it from the outside." He squeezed her knee gently, then opened his door and swung to the ground.

While he walked around the front of the truck, Stacy took a shaky breath and hastily released the seat belt. She knew what she had to do: get out of the truck without touching him, then keep her distance. It was obvious. It was also vital. Mac was in a dangerous mood and, unfortunately, she wasn't far behind him.

Mac threw open the door, wrapped his big hands around her waist and lifted her out, but instead of letting her down he held her right where she was, her breasts almost touching his chest, her eyes level with his.

"Kiss me, Stacy," he muttered, watching her eyes widen in alarm.

"Mac," she blurted out, "this isn't a good idea. Actually, it's a very bad idea. In fact, we'd have to look long and hard to find a worse idea."

"Please?" His fingers tightened around her waist.

Bracing her hands on his wide shoulders, shaken more than she would admit by the controlled hunger in his eyes, she took a ragged breath and slowly shook her head.

Mac brought her about an inch closer. "See?" he said against her lips, a thread of laughter in his murmur, "Saying *please* just doesn't work with a stubborn woman."

The kiss lasted only a second, was barely more than a brush of his lips against hers, but it was long enough for her hands to tangle in his hair, for Stacy to feel her nipples bead to aching points against his hard chest. Long enough to taste coffee and desire on his lips, long enough to be swamped by his heat, the lingering scent of soap and something clean and fresh that reminded her of tall mountains and the wind rustling through the cottonwoods. Something that belonged only to Mac.

"Mac." She blinked at the sound of her shaken whisper. "Put me down, please."

Dropping a swift, hard kiss on her parted lips, he turned and took a long step away from the door. Instead of being lowered to the ground as she'd expected, Stacy found herself dropped none too gently on the front fender of the truck. She gasped as her bottom hit the warm metal, and almost choked when Mac moved in close between her parted knees.

Too close.

So close that the buttons on his shirt pressed through the flimsy material of her blouse into her overheated flesh. So close that the solid evidence of his arousal was boldly imprinted on her belly.

Instinctively Stacy tightened her knees and groaned when they clenched around his muscular buttocks, pulling him even closer.

She looked up into hot, dark eyes and knew that no one had ever wanted her the way that Mac McClain wanted her, right here and now. Right here beneath the sheltering piñon branches, on the fender of a truck.

Certainly not the young college man with whom she'd had a short-lived affair in her sophomore year. Nor had the second one, several years later. And there had been no others, before or since.

Mac made her feel like a fragile and precious gift about to be unwrapped, like a desirable, feminine, sexy-as-hell woman. And she was learning—too quickly— that a woman's feelings ran as hot and wild as a man's. When his lips brushed hers, she murmured a shaky protest, shuddering when he drew her closer into the curve of his hard body.

Swamped by his silent demands and her own blood coursing through her veins like fire, Stacy buried her face in Mac's chest, flinching when he moved convulsively against her.

"Mac," she groaned, "I can't do this."

"You can do any damn thing you want to do." His voice was a deep rumble that she felt against her cheek. His arms tightened around her until she could hardly breathe.

"No." Her voice was muffled against his shirt. "I really can't."

The situation had exploded out of control too quickly for her to be afraid, but now Stacy waited, tense with sudden worry, confronting the realization that women have dealt with through the ages—she was no physical match for the man who held her. If she had to fight, she had little chance of winning. He had all the advantages—height, weight and awesome strength developed by a lifetime of hard physical work. Holding her breath, she hoped that his control was as powerful as the hunger shuddering through his big body. Long before her anxiety became outright fear, she learned that it was.

Barely.

Exhaling sharply, Mac dropped his hands to her thighs and gazed down at her. The glimmer of apprehension in her green eyes seared him like a rope burn. What the hell was he doing to her? To both of them? He swore softly, taking a deep breath and staring up through the branches to the blue sky above, trying to tamp down the fire raging through his body. He had never forced a woman in his life, but both of them knew that he had come damn close to it this time.

He swore again, calling himself every name in the book and some that had never made it. He had barged into her life and between her legs and probably scared her to death, put her off men for the rest of her life. She had enough sizzle in her delicate body to start a forest fire, but she was too small, too vulnerable to be handled like that.

Mac felt sweat trickling down his cheeks. He was still hot, harder than he was hot, and still pressed against her slender body. He had to move, back up, give her some room, let her put those silky thighs together and pretend that a wild man hadn't broken through one of society's polite barriers. And he would. Soon. Any minute now. Only two things were holding him back. She felt so damn good he never wanted to move, and when he did move he'd have to look in those trusting eyes that gazed right through a man. And he didn't want to see what he deserved to see.

Her tentative wiggle brought him back with a snap, and his hands tightened on her thighs. "Uh, Stacy, sweetheart, will you just . . . not move for a little bit?"

"I'm just trying to—"

"I know. No, don't. Just . . . give me a minute here, okay? It feels so . . . damn . . . good."

She looked at him helplessly.

His gaze snagged hers, and if he could have moved, the expression he saw would have sent him to his knees. There was none of the shock he'd expected, not even anger. He blinked thoughtfully, studying her vivid face. Embarrassment was there, adding a bit of pink to her golden tan, but overriding that was surprise and, yes, dammit, pleasure. For a second she looked like a kitten licking cream off its whiskers.

Mac knew he had never enjoyed anything so much in his life. If he couldn't make love with Stacy, watching her trying to sort things out came a close second. Expectancy and sheer, flaming curiosity widened her eyes. But what kept him pressed against her, hard and hurting, was the sense of anticipation, intrigue and dangerous fascination that shimmered through her slight body.

He hoped to God that she never wanted to try a high-stakes game in Vegas, because she'd lose everything she had, including her sweet tush. He'd never known anyone, even a ten-year-old kid, with such a revealing face. She thought of something and presto, it was there for all the world to see. Absently he made a mental note to keep her away from the bunkhouse poker games.

"Uh, Mac?"

"Yeah?"

"I think we ought to—"

"'Yeah, I know." But still he stood there, flexing his fingers on the resilient flesh of her thighs.

She took a ragged breath and let it out on a long sigh. "I hate to sound like a small-town country girl, but what's happening here? One minute we were talking and the next ... this." A vague gesture with her hand indicated the two of them and the truck.

Mac, thinking about moving, said vaguely, "Maybe it's just that old devil sex."

"I'd call it temporary insanity," Stacy stated firmly.

"Think about it this way," he suggested, giving himself a few more seconds. "You've got a living, breathing invitation to excitement and adventure. Right here. All you can handle."

Stacy drew in a breath, but it wasn't until he saw her eyes narrow with sudden temper that Mac knew he was in trouble.

"Is that what this is about?" she demanded wrathfully. "You think I'm out prowling the roads looking for a man?" She tried to lash out at him with her foot, but quickly saw the difficulty of kicking a man whose body was planted between her legs. Instead, she satisfied her instinct for battle by thumping him on the chest with the side of her fist.

"You are dense, you know it? Really stupid. Well, don't do the small-town spinster any favors, okay, McClain? The last thing in the world I want is a complication like this. Get away from me, you ... throwback to a Neanderthal!" Furiously she scooted back and pushed against his chest at the same time. "And before you even ask—no, men are not on my list!"

Mac moved away a lot faster than he had intended, getting well away from the lethal lashing of her feet. If the expression on her face was any indication, she was not in the mood for a meaningful discussion.

"No men?" he repeated, setting her off again.

"None," she assured him, her voice reeking with feminine satisfaction. "No men or man, singular or plural. Why should they be on there? My trip is supposed to be fun. Why would I deliberately get tangled up with someone who's bigheaded and hardheaded and nothing but trouble?"

Stacy slid off of the fender, glaring up at Mac. "Well, are you or are you not going to show me the ranch?"

"Calm down, spitfire." Mac touched her elbow, nudging her toward a worn path through the trees. "I wasn't insulting you."

"Could have fooled me," she muttered, jerking her arm away from his hand.

His voice hardened. "I was making an offer. You say you're looking for excitement, right?"

She gave him a grudging nod.

"Well, from what I've seen today, we could whip up as much as either one of us could handle. Probably more."

"Mac." She gave a long-suffering sigh. "I'm not talking about sex, for heaven's sake. I'm talking about..." She threw up her hands in exasperation. "I feel like I'm talking to a fence post. Will you listen? I'm referring to new experiences, things that will enrich my life."

They stepped out of the trees into a clearing that led to a lookout point. As they walked toward it, Mac said calmly, "I think when we go to bed together, it will be a new experience. For both of us. And who knows, it might even turn out to be enriching." He stopped her with a hand on her shoulder, pointing ahead. "That's McClain Butte, my western boundary."

"Mac, that's miles away! You can't own all of this. It's indecent. And you shouldn't be naming mountains after yourself."

"Butte," he corrected, "and it's named after my great-great-grandfather. He was one of the original settlers in the area and he bought every square inch of land he could afford. Each generation following him did the same."

"That's one heck of a legacy," she said softly, looking out over the vista. The sun was dropping fast, spreading long, dark shadows by the trees and spreading a golden nimbus along the distant peaks.

"We'd better get back," Mac said a few minutes later. "It'll be dark soon. I'm driving over to the eastern section tomorrow afternoon. Want to come along?"

"No, thank you," Stacy said politely, obediently retracing her steps. "I'm going to be looking for my power place."

The drive back to the house was a quiet one. Stacy sat close to the door, clutching the handle when the truck bounced over potholes. She looked thoughtful, Mac reflected. Probably thinking about that mysterious list of hers.

He spent a few minutes considering it himself, but his mind always circled back to the same question.

What the hell was a power place?

Five

Déjà vu, Stacy thought morosely the next day at the supper table. Once again ten men were looking at her in baffled disbelief, and the eleventh, having started the whole thing, sat back and watched, his eyes never leaving her face.

"Well," Red drawled doubtfully, "there's those power lines up on the southern slope."

Slim shook his head. "Tumbleweed don't ride, remember? And she'd play merry hell getting up there any other way. I think she'd be better off with the generators in the tool shed."

Stacy turned an exasperated face toward Mac, narrowing her eyes when he grinned. But it was the thoughtful, patient expression behind the smile that bothered her, she realized an instant later, trying to shake off the frisson of alarm creeping up her spine. It reminded her of...of Gibraltar. The rock. He had the look of a man who plans and moves with great deliberation, one who leaves nothing to chance. No, he was definitely not the impulsive type, she thought for the hundredth time.

Stacy looked down at her plate, wondering if she could be mistaken. She doubted it. She had learned a long time ago that her instincts with people were usually right on the mark. But if they were now, with Mac, then what about yesterday? Had he planned to haul her out of the truck, plunk her on the fender and hold her until he drove both breath and reason out of her body?

No. She didn't know how she knew with such certainty, but she knew. He hadn't. He hadn't been tormenting her, he honestly had not been able to move away.

Dazed by the sudden realization that he'd had little or no more control over yesterday's events than she had, Stacy took in a shuddering breath. While the conversation about power sources bounced around the table like a Ping-Pong ball, she shot him a speculative glance. She immediately wished she hadn't.

Mac's dark gaze was still on her, reminding her of a large cat watching a mouse hole. It worried her, that look. He seemed to have placed her in the category of a puzzle to be solved. A puzzle to which he was willing to devote an inordinate amount of attention. Yes indeedy, she decided with a sigh, it worried her.

"Wait a minute, guys," she said, waving her hands to get their attention. "Mac didn't mean I was looking for electricity." When they turned to look at her, she drew in a deep breath that seemed loud in the sudden silence. "It's not that at all. It's something . . . invisible." She scanned their blank faces and tried again. "It's something...emanating from the earth...that gives you power," she ended feebly.

Mel, a lean, dark man who had never done more than nod a greeting, broke the silence. "Oh, God," he groaned, "I left Los Angeles to get away from talk like that."

"Is this one of those tree hugger things?" Slim asked.

"Wait a minute, let me read it to you." Stacy rushed into the living room and retrieved her book. Sitting back down, she thumbed through the pages, muttering under her breath. "Okay, listen up. It says right here that a power spot is a place that you're drawn to, it gives you a sense of personal power. It can be just a matter of a few feet in size or many miles long."

She scanned the rest of the page before looking up. "It's a concentration of energy. A vortex or an energy spring. I've read that there's a number of them in the Sedona area."

"Sedona?" Curly's voice broke the silence. "You mean the place where people wear crystals and sit out on the rocks looking for UFOs?"

"Some of them," Stacy admitted, watching the men exchange glances. "Very few," she added firmly, wondering a bit wildly how the conversation had strayed to outer space. Bringing it firmly back to the point at hand, she waggled the book so they could all see the title. "You guys may think I'm a little off center here, but I believe in these things and I'm going to keep on looking until I find one for myself. Just so I'll know the feeling. That way, I'll recognize it when I come across it in California."

She wasn't surprised when Mac scowled. The man had a knee-jerk reaction to his neighboring state, she reflected. Every time she mentioned it, he glowered. "If it'll make you feel any better," she added with a grin, "the first time I heard about power spots was in a self-defense class, so I'm not really hanging out there in left field with the fringe element. Apparently it's something you either believe in or you don't."

She took a swallow of coffee, trying not to smile as she eyed their carefully expressionless faces over the rim of the cup. "I'll just check out a few places around here and see what happens," she told them. "I have plenty of time, and if I find anything interesting, I'll let you know. And speaking of time," she said, abruptly turning to Curly, "have you heard anything about my car?"

"Not me." He stared at Mac with an over-to-you expression. "Boss?"

Mac shook his head. "Pete'll probably call in the morning," he told Stacy. "As soon as he does, I'll get you so you can talk to him."

"Hey, Tumbleweed, how you going to know this place if you do find it?" Slim asked, curiosity overcoming his skepticism. "Will it look different?"

Stacy gave a small shrug, knowing her reply would generate another round of wooden expressions. "I doubt it. I'll probably just feel it."

She was right. Slim opened his mouth, changed his mind and closed it. Just then Maxie came in with a pie in each hand, and Red and Doc jumped up to help her.

For the next few minutes the men ate in appreciative silence, carefully avoiding Stacy's gaze. As soon as they could, they filed out the door muttering their good-nights.

Maxie refilled Stacy's cup and set the coffeepot near Mac. She touched Stacy's shoulder, keeping her in her chair. "You finish your pie and don't even think of coming in the kitchen. You did more than your share this afternoon. Mac, don't let her get up, hear me? Those boys keep her talking and don't let her eat enough to fill a mosquito. You watch her now, otherwise she'll be leaving here skinnier than a rail."

She waited to see if either of them planned to argue, then tucked the stack of plates against her hipbone and straight-armed her way through the swinging door.

Looking at the slab of apple pie before her, Stacy took a bite and chewed thoughtfully. "You two aren't related, are you?"

Mac leaned back in his chair, a glimmer of amusement in his eyes. "Actually, we are. Second cousins, I think. See a resemblance, do you?"

"Bossy," she said succinctly. "You think you know what's best for everyone and you make no bones about telling them." Giving the remaining portion of pie a look of regret, she placed her fork on the plate.

"And what's more," he said blandly, "we're usually right." He grinned and held up a hand in a peaceful gesture when she shot him an indignant look. "Stacy, a ranch is a business, not a democracy. When I hire a hand, he doesn't expect to get a vote. He's free to offer suggestions, but I make the decisions and he follows orders."

"Business I understand," she assured him. "I just think it's carrying things a bit far when it slides over into your personal life. It's not an endearing trait in a relationship."

His brows rose. "You think I do that?"

"I know you do. The hat business," she reminded him. "You said, here it is. Wear it. Or else. It lacked a certain element of charm."

"I wanted to make sure that you didn't keel over from heat exhaustion," he told her, a muscle in his jaw tightening. "And I didn't want to argue about it."

"That's just the point," she said serenely. "I might not have argued. You had no way of knowing how I'd react if you simply explained and asked. You just assumed I'd give you a bad time."

Mac leaned back and studied her, his eyes gleaming with interest. "Is that what we have, a relationship?"

"It was just a figure of speech," she replied hastily, blinking at the sudden tension in the room. "I was simply making a point."

"You think I'd be that way with a lover?" he asked bluntly.

"Yep." Although her heart jumped at both the question and the image it presented, she nodded. He wasn't going to get off that easily. "*And* with a wife. You'd probably get away with it, too, if you married a doormat." His eyes narrowed, and before she lost her nerve, she added blithely, "But I'd sure like to be around for the fireworks if you didn't. Marry a doormat, I mean." She paused a beat. "Then again, maybe I wouldn't. I don't even like to watch violent films."

"Are you saying you think I'd abuse a woman?"

"No. Absolutely not!" She shook her head and was momentarily blinded by her hair. "That's not what I meant." Her response was as swift as it was sincere, and he slowly relaxed, the shocked fury fading from his eyes. She grinned at him. "I just think you'd be arrogant, high-handed and pushy."

"Thanks. For nothing."

"Just the way you were tonight," she added. "Throwing me to the wolves with this power place business. Why did you have to say anything to them?"

Mac gave an exasperated sigh. "Because they were worried about you. You spent most of the day wandering around like you were lost, stopping on a dime and standing so still you looked rooted. They thought something was wrong."

"Oh." Stacy looked disconcerted as she pushed her chair back from the table.

Mac tilted his head toward the kitchen where Maxie was clattering dishes and pans then pointed to her plate. "You know what she'll say if you don't finish that."

"Mac, I love your second cousin dearly, but I refuse to be bullied—about food or anything else." She picked up the plate and headed for the kitchen, her eyes revealing her anticipation for the oncoming battle. Looking over her shoulder, she said, "Don't come in unless you see blood seeping under the door."

Half an hour later, Mac sat in his office watching Stacy through the window. In her hot-pink walking shorts and screaming turquoise shirt she was hard to miss, but he knew he would have spotted her even if she'd been wearing camouflage in a jungle. Book in hand, she was wandering toward the barn, stopping every now and then, apparently in deep communion with the patch of ground beneath her feet. She rarely made a move these days without an audience, he reflected wryly, and tonight was no exception. Red and Slim leaned against the corral fence, involved in an elaborate conversation, pretending not to watch her stop-and-go progress.

Keeping Stacy in view, Mac leaned back in his swivel chair and propped his booted feet on the corner of the scarred, massive, oak desk, his heels resting on a stack of papers. He nudged the latest batch of government forms aside with disgust. Damned things multiplied like sand fleas, and they came through the mail with the regularity of a revolving door. As soon as one quarterly report was sent in, another came, gathering dust until it was time to fill *that* one out. And they were as confusing as a Chinese puzzle, as complex as . . .

Mac's eyes narrowed in speculation. As complex as a woman who pulled up her roots, left everything familiar behind and struck out on her own. A woman with no specific destination and no goals other than to find excitement. And in her case, probably trouble. What else could happen when a small-town innocent was turned loose among some of those California crazies? His stomach knotted at the thought.

Stacy was like a hawk riding the lift of a thermal, chasing freedom. And while she was airborne, would she head for some underpopulated area smelling of sweet grass and tall trees? Hell no. Knowing her, she'd drop right down in the middle of Los Angeles and every con man, drug dealer and pimp in a fifty-mile area would zero in on her.

Mac's face grew grim. She wouldn't have a chance.

He was wrong about one thing, he decided abruptly. She was no hawk. Not a raptor. Never that. Hell, she didn't even know how to defend herself, in spite of those self-defense classes she kept talking about. Yesterday, sitting on that fender, she'd been as open and helpless as a babe, all wide eyes and pounding heart. And parted lips. And soft sounds in the back of her throat.

No, definitely not a hawk. She was more like a hummingbird, fragile, colorful, hovering and gone in a flash. Even her CB handle was wrong, he decided. She might be gallivanting around on her own, but she was no tumbleweed. There was nothing sere or withered about her. She was spring itself. A sprite, overflowing with zest.

Mac blinked thoughtfully. She was also a woman who called herself a small-town spinster. A woman who had looked astounded when he'd told her she was sexy. A woman who didn't believe it.

Why?

Sighing, he briefly closed his eyes and shook his head, knowing that question would join the others that had kept him awake for the last two nights. Why was Stacy wandering around on her own? Why wasn't there a man hot on her trail? Why did she have everything she owned packed in a car? What was on that famous list she kept talking about?

And why was he concentrating on a sprite in hot-pink shorts when he could be looking for a wife?

Swearing softly, Mac pushed back from the desk, his feet hitting the floor with a thud. Because, dammit, in the last two days everything had changed. When he pictured a wife, he saw Stacy, a woman blazing with life, a woman with dreams, a woman on the run. When he thought of a family, he saw a batch of kids with tousled brown hair, kids dressed in blinding colors running around the place.

Moving swiftly, he headed for the front of the house. Stacy had angled away from the barn, and he vaulted the picket fence, cutting her off. "Stacy! Hold on, I want to show you something."

She looked over her shoulder and slowed down. "I thought you were in the office keeping the IRS at bay."

He shrugged. "They're always there, I'm always here. It can wait. Come on, this way."

Stacy stopped, giving him a suspicious look. "Why?

"Why what?" he asked blandly. His hand at her elbow urged her on.

"Okay, I'll come, but it won't work," she assured him after a moment's thought, moving reluctantly beside him. Her hair danced around her face when she looked up at him, then slid back in place like a silky cap. "Whatever gruesome thing you've cooked up to distract me. I paid six ninety-five for this book. It's an interesting idea, and I'm having fun looking around."

"I'm not trying to stop you." He reached down and lightly clasped her hand, lacing his fingers through hers. "I just want you to take a break. Trust me on this one. You can start again tomorrow."

He wasn't about to discourage her, Mac reflected. The longer she scouted around looking for nonexistent power places, the less she worried about her car and how long it was taking to get back on the road. With any luck at all, he might be able to stall her a week or so, or at least long enough for her to...

To what? he wondered. Change her mind about leaving? Decide that a ranch a hundred miles from civilization was as exciting as bright lights and weirdos? Come to his bed, her green eyes gleaming with curiosity and enthusiasm? He swore again, silently, stalking beside her, deliberately turning his thoughts to the IRS and their latest batch of cryptic forms until the gathering tension in his body eased.

They followed the worn path that led over the tree-studded hill behind the house, past tangles of manzanita and scrub oak, beyond a clutch of boulders and down toward the shade of several large cottonwoods. "All right," Mac said, squeezing her hand, "shut your eyes and let me lead you in."

Eyes closed, Stacy stepped forward, stiffening slightly when Mac's arm circled her waist. "Relax," he murmured, tightening his arm. "I've got you."

That's exactly what she was worried about. She didn't *want* him to have her. Not here. Not now.

Not yet.

She stepped forward, flinching when the shadows overhead turned the gold against her eyelids to black. She hadn't bargained on meeting a man, Stacy acknowledged silently, forcing herself to relax, allowing Mac to draw her against his hard body when the path slanted downward. Especially before the Kansas dust had even settled behind her flying car. Oddly enough, she hadn't even thought of a man. And that was *very* odd, she supposed, considering that many women in her age group were starkly contemplating both their unmarried states and the countdown of their biological clocks.

But this was to have been a golden time, she reminded herself. A time for fun, to explore the unknown, to discover new horizons, form a new life-style. A time to fly, to be free. A time, she had always understood, that would inevitably end, somehow leaving her changed. How much or how little remained to be seen.

And if she *had* pictured a man, complete with a happy-ever-after ending, she would never have visualized one like Mac. She couldn't have, Stacy reflected wryly, for the simple reason that her imagination wasn't that vivid. It was also a fact that while she had granted herself both time and permission to have an adventure, the woman beneath the impetuous facade was depressingly practical. If she had been asked to describe her ideal man, she would have started with traits that could also portray a family pet: loyal and devoted.

Sensations crowded in on her, scattering her thoughts, leaving her skin prickly and her lungs oxygen starved. First the heat of Mac's big body brushing hers, the tangy scents of his recent shave and shower, mingled with dust and pine needles. Then the strobelike effect of sunshine and shadow against her eyelids and her bare arms and legs. The whisper of the wind through the leafy cottonwoods meshed with the cool tumble of water over rocks.

"Hold on," Mac said, bringing her to a halt. He scooped her up in his arms, saying, "This is a little tricky. Keep your eyes closed." Startled, Stacy clutched his shoulders and hesitantly looped her arms around his neck, tightening them as he half slid, half slithered down a steep incline. It was so quiet she could hear pebbles bouncing and the snap of dry pine needles.

"Mac," she protested breathlessly, "what on earth are you doing?"

"You'll see. Just another couple of seconds." His arms tightened around her as leaves skimmed her hair. Instinctively, she raised her hand to ward them off. "You're okay," he told her again, his voice calm. "I've got you."

He settled her on a thick tree limb, steadying her as her fingers clutched the front of his shirt. With her free hand she clung to the branch. "Mac—"

"Now. Look."

Stacy opened her eyes and looked directly into his. He was standing in front of her, boxing her in with a hand braced on either side of her thighs. She was right, she thought, they were black. His eyes were so dark she couldn't distinguish the pupils. And hot. Possession gleamed in them, and outright hunger.

He stepped to one side, one arm propped on the limb next to her thigh. With his free hand he gestured, inviting her inspection. "What do you think?"

Her swift, circling glance took in the silvery green leaves rustling overhead, the dappled shadows, the curving path behind them and the creek below. Water, pure and clear, broke over colorful, glistening rocks tumbled smooth by time and weather. When her gaze touched his face, he was waiting, his wonderful, incredibly sexy mouth smiling.

"It's magical," she said slowly, absorbing the astonishing beauty of the grotto. "A place to dream."

He made a satisfied sound deep in his throat. "I thought you'd like it."

"Like it?" She looked at him in disbelief. "Mac, you don't just *like* a place like this. You treasure it. You absorb it into your very soul, and most of all, you preserve it." She put one hand on his shoulder and the other on the branch, bracing herself while she scooted forward. Bark scraped the back of her knees and thighs. "Ouch." She winced. "Help me, Mac. Please. I want to get down by the water."

Mac wrapped his hands around her waist and lifted her, holding her against him for a long moment. Then with a sharp sigh, he lowered her, groaning when her breasts brushed his chest.

Gasping at the touch, shocked by the heat and hardness of his big body, Stacy broke away as soon as her toes touched the ground, darting the few feet to the water's edge. "Oh, Mac, just look at this, it's beautiful." She was babbling, she knew, sounding idiotic, but it was better than standing frozen, staring at him with a silent invitation in her eyes.

Water flowed out of the hill, bubbling and frothing around an angled series of enormous flat rocks that looked like a giant's spiral staircase. Turning back to Mac, who was slowly following, she asked, "Where does it come from?"

"Underground spring. It flows all year-round."

Stacy nodded absently, looking down to check her sneakers. If she slipped, a little water wouldn't hurt them, she decided. With no more thought than that, she launched herself off the path to the first boulder. It was smooth, dry, flat and big enough to use for a picnic.

For the next few minutes she climbed the rocks, delighting in every discovery, eventually circling out of sight of the man who watched her from the shadows. She poked and prodded crevices and finally reached the top, dipping her hand in to test the temperature of the water when she discovered a pool about the size of a hot tub. Chilly, but not freezing, she decided, giving it a critical glance. And the clear water would come to just about her waist. The bottom was strewn with sand and the same small, colorful river rocks that lined the creek bed.

Stacy worked her way back down to the lowest level, giving an exultant laugh when she leapt from the last boulder to the path. The air locked in her lungs when Mac caught her, swinging her around in his arms. When her feet touched the ground, he held her, drawing her closer, slowly, giving her time to protest.

She didn't. She couldn't. They had come too close to this, too many times. She needed him the same way she needed air. Her eyes met his in a long look and she shivered, knowing that she was as hungry as he was.

"Do I stop?" he muttered, brushing his warm lips against hers.

"Oh, I hope not," she replied with shattering honesty. When he smiled, tightening his arms around her, her heart thudded at the proprietary gleam in his eyes and she took a ragged breath, framing his cheeks with her hands. "We're talking kisses here," she warned breathlessly, "not lifetime commitments. Not even five minutes from now."

Her thumb touched his bottom lip, and she blinked. It was warm and moist and far softer than she expected. "But right now I need your lips on mine more than I've ever needed anyth—"

All waiting over, he yanked her closer, until she could hardly breathe. Then his mouth came down on hers, swamping her senses.

Stacy clutched at Mac's shoulders, nestling closer following him as he leaned back against a tree trunk. She was drawn into the cradle of his parted legs, off balance, trusting him to support her, fully aware of the swift arousal of the body beneath hers.

Six

On one level, Stacy knew that she was taking an incredible risk, that she should move, back away, make at least a halfhearted protest. But at that moment, more than anything, she needed to feel Mac's heat, to savor his hands moving over her and to feel his body hard against hers. She slid her hands behind his neck, lacing her fingers in his thick hair. "Ah, Mac, you feel so good."

"I've been waiting for this since I saw you perched on the hood of that damned car." He brushed his lips over hers, his fingers kneading a heated trail down her back. He kissed her throat, then delicately grazed her earlobe with his teeth, groaning encouragement when she shuddered. "Kiss me, honey. Lean on me. Closer. Burn me up with all that fire."

Fire? she wondered, tightening her fingers in his hair. Yes, it was there, searing her, following the path his hand made from her breast to her belly. She gave in to the excitement he stirred so easily in her, and with a moan of growing passion, opened her mouth and invited him in.

Mac instantly accepted. He touched the tip of her tongue with his, then deepened the kiss while his hands moved beneath her shirt and dealt with the fragile barrier of her bra, stripping both of them off and tossing them aside. He lifted her higher, looking down past green eyes heavy with wonder and wanting to the soft curves of her breasts. When he touched her beaded nipple with the tip of his tongue, she shuddered.

Excitement poured through him. She wanted him. Hell, she was damn near burning up with it. "Unbutton my shirt," he muttered urgently. "I've got to feel you against me."

Stacy's fingers shook so, it took forever. Mac didn't help her. He swore silently when she fumbled with the buttons, but he waited, his gaze locked on her face. She looked like she was opening a damn Christmas present, he thought, feeling his body grow harder as he watched her curious green eyes widen in anticipation.

Stacy ripped apart the two halves of his open shirt, pulling them loose from his belt. Her hands seemed to work with a will of their own, her palms sliding over the crisp mat of hair, her fingertips tempting a flat nipple out of hiding.

"Yeah," Mac groaned. "Don't stop... Oh, honey, that's pure, sweet torture. Come here." He pulled her closer, until she couldn't breathe, couldn't think.

One large hand held her head still for his mouth. He captured her lips again, and Stacy sighed as his free hand glided up her rib cage and cupped her breast with a tenderness unexpected in such a large man. "Oh, Mac." He held her the way he would hold a bird, she thought dazedly. Gentling her, showing her that she was safe in his hands.

When his palm touched her belly, she made a purring sound deep in her throat. A second later, when his fingers worked at the buttons on her shorts, her common sense kicked in. "Mac, uh, I don't think... Mac, *no!*"

He wasn't called Gibraltar because he was slow, she reminded herself, blinking up at his taut face. She had learned that much about him in the past two days. She was in the arms of a man who always knew where he was going and, one way or another, usually got there. So if she had any objections, she'd better state them now and make them loud and clear.

"No," she repeated, shaking her head as she tried to lever herself off him. It wasn't easy, and he wasn't helping. Mac's hands were still clasping her waist, holding her hips against his, and for a second she knew it was touch and go.

"Dammit!" he muttered urgently. "I want you, Stacy. More than I've ever wanted anyone in my life. And you want me." He slid his fingers into the back pockets of her shorts, keeping her where she was.

Stacy cleared her throat and looked down, realizing for the first time that she was naked. Half-naked. *Where on earth were her clothes?* The sudden and vibrant awareness of her bare breasts pulled her even further out of the sensual haze she'd been wrapped in.

"You're right, I do want you," she admitted huskily. Not as much as she had thirty seconds earlier, but she wanted him.

Mac groaned and eased his hands out of her pockets, smoothing his warm palms down the curve of her bottom. "Do I hear a *but* here?"

Stacy sighed, resting her cheek on his bare chest, wiggling her bottom a bit to see if she was free. "Yeah, you do. Several of them. *But* we've only known each other less than forty-eight hours. *But* I'm going to be leaving in a few days. *But* I don't do one-night stands or affairs. *But* I don't even do this kind of thing."

"What kind of thing?" A wry grin tugged at his lips.

"Fall into a man's arms with half my clothes off," she said absently, looking around with a frown. "Dammit, Mac, where are they?"

He nodded toward the right. "Over there. On the bush."

She scrambled to her feet, feeling the heat in her cheeks. It would be nice if she could carry this off with just a modicum of poise, she thought grimly, turning her back to Mac and giving her bra a vigorous shake before she slipped it on. It would be *very* nice, but she wasn't going to count on it. She had a strong feeling that her face was as red as it was hot.

"Darn it, Mac, these could have fallen in the water."

"They would have dried."

"They're probably covered with ticks."

"I'll be glad to do a body check tonight."

"And some of the men could have wandered up here and found us. Talk about embarrassing," she mumbled, pulling the shirt over her head.

"No."

"What do you mean *no?*" Stacy turned around and found her nose almost pressed against Mac's bare chest. "Do you have to creep up on people like that?" Her heart thudded, and she gave him an annoyed glance, hastily tucking her shirt inside her shorts.

"I mean no they wouldn't have found us," he said calmly. "Because they never come up here. This is my place. The only people who come here are invited."

"I wasn't," she said stubbornly.

Mac sighed. "You're really looking for a fight, aren't you? I brought you here, didn't I? If you want it formal, you've got it. You're welcome to visit my hideaway any time you want to come, for as long as you want to stay."

He buttoned his shirt and gazed thoughtfully at her flushed face. "Do you think I'd allow you to be embarrassed by any of the men like that?"

"Oh." Gibraltar, she reminded herself. A man who planned ahead, a man who covered all contingencies. "It's going to be dark pretty soon," she blurted out, refusing to look at him. She fussed with the sleeve of her shirt, smoothing out an imaginary wrinkle, thinking again about poise. Too late, she decided gloomily, she had already blown it. Mac, on the other hand, was calmly tucking in his shirt, acting as if he did this sort of thing every day.

"We'd better get back to the house," she said abruptly. She spun around, forcing herself to a deliberate pace, half convinced that if she ran, Mac would be all over her like a second skin. As it was, he was right on her heels.

"Stacy?"

"What?"

"It's okay, honey." His large hand cupped her shoulder and drew her back against him.

"Sure." And pigs could fly. *Nothing* was okay. She shrugged, frowning when his hand stayed where it was.

"There's nothing to be embarrassed about."

"I'm not." Embarrassed didn't even come close, she decided. Try flustered. Try disconcerted. Try *mortified*. In all of her twenty-seven years she had never thrown herself at a man. Especially not the way she'd just thrown herself at Mac. She had never tried to tear off a man's shirt, either. Walking briskly, she refused to consider what else she hadn't done before today.

"Stacy?"

"What?" She gave him a frazzled look.

"Do you have any idea how beautiful you are?"

Startled, she waited just a beat too long before saying in a coolly polite voice, "Thank you, Mac. It's very nice of you to say so."

"But you don't believe a word I'm saying?"

Stacy hurried down the path, breathing a grateful sigh when they crested the hill and looked down on the house. She didn't want to answer his question any more than she wanted to consider what emotions might be lurking behind his placid voice. "Look." She pointed down to the yard, grateful for the distraction. "There's Maxie. Do you suppose she's looking for us?"

When Mac gave a shrill whistle, Maxie shaded her eyes and looked up the hill. She waved, put a clenched fist to her mouth and one to her ear, then pointed to the house.

"Telephone," Mac said, grabbing Stacy's hand and dragging her along. He took off at an easy lope, adjusting his stride to her shorter one.

"Pete's on the phone," Maxie called when Mac stepped over the picket fence, well away from the gate. She waited while he scooped Stacy up and set her down next to him before adding, "He wants to talk to Stacy. Hope you're ready for a long visit, kiddo. He didn't sound like he had good news. Come on, grab it in the kitchen before he hangs up."

A few minutes later Stacy cradled the phone and turned to face Mac and Maxie. Both of them were leaning against the counter, arms crossed on their chests, watching her. They had been listening to every word of the one-sided conversation.

"Ten days," she said blankly.

"All right!" Maxie jabbed a clenched fist high in the air.

"At the earliest."

"What'd he say the problem was?" Mac asked.

Stacy waved a vague hand. "Pretty much what you suspected. A computerized whatsit that seems to affect every vital organ. He said it'll be simple enough to replace. Once they get the part."

"They usually are."

Maxie winced. "It'll probably cost the earth."

"That's not the problem." Stacy perched on the corner of the table, absently swinging her feet. "It's under warranty. It's just the time involved. Pete's local guy has to order it." She shook her head. "I don't understand it. How can they run a store without keeping parts in stock?"

Mac shrugged. "It's happening more all the time. Companies don't want their money tied up in inventory."

"It's stupid," Stacy said flatly. "They could go out of business that way."

"Not out here. They don't have a whole lot of competition, so they can do pretty much what they want."

Stacy studied her shoes for a long moment, then looked up. "Mac—"

"Don't even start." His eyes narrowed in a sudden frown and he gave her a long, level look. A dangerous look, full of warning. "You know you're welcome to stay. If you went anywhere else, you'd just be sitting in a motel room while you waited.''

"But—"

Maxie gave her boss a thoughtful glance before she turned to Stacy. "Look at it this way," she soothed. "We've got a million flat rocks out there you can meditate on. And there'll be plenty of time for you to find both your inner woman *and* your power spot. What more can you ask for?"

"But I shouldn't—"

"Wouldn't you rather be here?" Mac asked bluntly, moving toward the back door.

"Well, yes, but—"

"Fine. It's settled." He stopped and looked at her over his shoulder. "If you can't handle the good-neighbor policy, then keep on helping Maxie fix supper."

It wasn't the good-neighbor policy that bothered her, Stacy thought the following afternoon as she made her way up the path to Mac's hideaway. Nor was it the work. She enjoyed the time she spent in the kitchen with Mac's outspoken second cousin twice removed. Maxie had explained the twice removed business at length while she mixed up mounds of biscuit dough. She'd even sprinkled flour on the counter and drawn a chart of the McClain family tree.

The relation was a bit confusing, but one thing had come across loud and clear. Mac's family had been in the area forever, and Mac's family would continue to be in the area forever.

Just like the people in Kansas.

They were settled, they had their place in life, and there wasn't anything they wanted bad enough to go chasing around the country looking for it.

Mac, according to Maxie, was long overdue to settle down. He'd fixed up his house and now all he needed was a woman. The right woman.

"I'm a woman." The sound of her own voice startled her.

Well, she was that all right, Stacy reflected as she jumped out to the first flat boulder hunkering in the water. If the last four years had given her any doubts about the matter, the few minutes in Mac's arms yesterday had settled them.

"I'm just not the *right* woman."

Maxie knew what she was talking about, Stacy decided, peering over the far edge of the huge rock to the frothy water just inches below. Mac should have a woman. A wife. A mother for the children who would fill those empty bedrooms. Something bleak and cold clenched in her stomach at the thought, but after a long, desolate moment, she shrugged the feeling aside.

Not just any woman would do, she reflected stoically, sitting down on the sun-warmed rock to give the matter her full attention. He deserved someone special, someone anxious to put down roots, someone to live in the home surrounded by peaks and valleys. He needed a woman with spirit, one who could slug it out toe-to-toe with him and keep his Code-of-the-West complex from getting out of hand.

And one who was ready for commitment. Now. Not in six months or a year.

Stacy blinked and gazed up at the tree he had leaned against yesterday while he touched her with such rough care, his urgency, his need lighting a response in her that had, for an instant, been terrifying. She crossed her legs tailor-style and closed her eyes, determined to put the memory aside. The woman Mac needed should definitely have a fire to match his own.

Leaning against a high chunk of rock, she sighed as the warmth seeped into her back. Resting the backs of her hands against her knees, she took a deep breath and considered the matter, trying to be objective.

It wouldn't be easy, finding a woman like that. To begin with, she reflected, women weren't that plentiful out in the wilds a hundred miles from nowhere. And of those who were available, many of them had agendas of their own—a career, life in the fast lane, whatever.

No, it wouldn't be easy, she concluded with a small sigh. Drawing in a deep breath, she closed her eyes, reminding herself that anything worthwhile rarely came easily. What Mac needed ... Thoughts came and went, leaving no more impression than the sound of the rushing water tumbling and spilling over the warm rocks.

She was getting the hang of this meditation thing, she thought with satisfaction as her breathing slowed. The trick was to quit resisting, to let her thoughts flow, not force them or shut them out. And not to feel, not to be involved. If one corner of her mind insisted on chattering, it would gradually quiet. If she kept circling back to Mac, so be it.

Mac could take care of himself, she decided, inhaling slowly. He didn't need her or anyone else to solve his problems. What he *did* need was—

Stacy shook her head and firmly put him out of her mind. The discipline lasted for all of ten seconds.

What Mac needed was—

Stacy's eyes snapped open at the astonishing thought.

Her pulse rate shot up at the very idea, her internal alarm system a crazed mass of pealing bells and flashing red lights.

What Mac needed was Stacy Sullivan a year from now?

It makes sense, the crazy little voice inside her whispered. *You're already half in love with the man. and in a year—God willing—you'll have found what you're looking for. You'll have enough new faces and places stored up to last a lifetime. You'll travel as much as you want, find that inner woman you keep reading about and work through some of the items on that list of yours. Why not?*

Stacy blinked. Why not?

There were a hundred reasons.

A thousand.

A zillion, for God's sake!

In the first place, Mac wasn't a patient man. If he wanted a woman, he'd want her now, not in another year.

That's one. But it was a big one, Stacy thought, briefly closing her eyes. The only one that counted. Mac was ready to take the next step in his life. He wanted a wife and children. A woman only had to walk through his house to realize that.

So?

Her brows drew together in annoyance. So the timing was all wrong. She wasn't ready. She wanted all the things that Mac wanted, but not this very minute. Twice now, fate had barged in and changed her plans. She had worked long and hard to get to the point where she could call the shots in her own life, and she wasn't going to give it up. Not for Mac, not for anything.

For the first time she admitted exactly how vital this time was to her. If she was going to be successful in the next phase of her life—possibly as a wife and a mother, juggling a home and career—she had to know exactly what and how much she had missed along the way. The empty spaces had to be filled in before she would be whole.

And to bring anything less than a whole woman to a marriage was asking for trouble. It would be doomed before it began. Besides, Mac or any other man didn't deserve to be stuck with a woman who perpetually looked beyond the horizon thinking that she had to "find" herself.

But I was right about one thing, wasn't I? You are half in love with him, aren't you?

Stacy groaned and rolled over on her stomach, scooting to the edge of the boulder. Wrong, she thought, reaching down to scoop up a handful of polished, marble-size rocks. Dead wrong.

"Dammit," she said in a dazed voice. "I'm *all* the way in love with him."

She was perched on the highest of the rock stairs admiring her latest find—a small, amber, polished stone about the size of a pea—when she heard the men's voices. Before they came into sight, Mac called to her.

"Stacy, are you decent?"

"Of course I'm decent," she said indignantly, grateful that she hadn't given in to the impulse to go skinny-dipping. Actually, she was more than decent. If anything, her traveling clothes were a bit on the conservative side. Her walking shorts were all the same, brief enough to be cool, modest enough to wear comfortably in public. Some of her knit shirts had sleeves, some didn't. None were too tight or too short. But she *had* indulged herself when she'd selected the colors, she admitted. Vowing that she would never again wear beige, dark blue or black, she had headed straight for the most vivid shades in stock.

She looked down with a satisfied nod. Her raspberry pink outfit was one of her better choices, she reflected just as the two men emerged from the trees.

Mac scowled up at her. "Where's your hat?"

"Yes, it is a lovely day," she murmured. "And, thank you, I'm having a lovely time." Her comment didn't even slow Mac down, but his companion gave her a swift grin. "Good heavens," she said, taking a second look at the man standing beside Mac. He was almost as tall, almost as broad shouldered, with the same dark hair and devastating mouth. "Your parents had no mercy on the women around here. There're two of you."

"I'm Rick." The other one grinned up at her. "I got all the charm."

"Where...is...your...hat?" Mac's eyes narrowed with temper.

Stacy silently pointed to a tree stump.

"What the hell is it doing there?" Mac exploded. "You're supposed to wear—"

"Mac." Stacy looked upward in supplication. Deciding that no help was forthcoming from that direction, she scowled at him. "Am I or am I not sitting in the shade?"

"You are," Rick said helpfully.

"Can you come up with one solid reason why I should wear a hat in the shade?"

"Not me." Rick's smile broadened.

"You butt out," Mac said, not even looking at him.

"I wore the blasted hat when I left the house," Stacy pointed out in a martyred voice. "I wore it until I got here. I did what I agreed to do, so don't hassle me, McClain!" She turned away and dropped the amber rock in her pocket, adding it to the others she had found earlier.

"Who's the water sprite?" Rick asked.

"Stacy Sullivan," Mac said shortly. "She's staying here for a while."

"Who does she belong to?"

"She's mine."

Stacy felt her heart thud at the flat possession in Mac's voice, but the look she threw the men over her shoulder was one of sheer exasperation.

Rick grinned. "Does she know it?"

"Not yet, but she'll get the idea sooner or later."

"Too bad."

"Forget it, little brother. You're a day late and a dollar short."

Stacy scooted down the rocks until she stood level with them, separated by a narrow strip of running water. "Okay, you two, you've had your fun. I assume that was some form of Western humor, even if I didn't get the punch line. Now if you'll move, I'll jump across and retrieve my hat."

The two of them moved apart, each holding out a hand to her. As soon as Stacy clasped their hands, she was swung across the water and tucked into the space between them. Mac reached back, grabbed her hat and dropped it on her head.

Rick gave the brim a quick tug and smiled down into her startled eyes. "Just thought you'd like to know, Stacy Sullivan. Along with the charm, I got the sense of humor. My big brother always means what he says."

Seven

___

My big brother always means what he says.

Two nights later Stacy, wearing a purple jumpsuit that somehow soothed her jangled nerves, sat in the living room playing solitaire. The lamp hanging overhead cast a warm circle of light around the game table, the only light in the room other the blazing fire in the hearth.

Maxie closed the last window and shivered. "Darn! It's getting cold out there, and the wind's coming up. The rain will probably hit during the night."

Stacy looked up. "Is that good or bad on a ranch in July?"

"It depends. Good if you have the hay cut, baled and covered. Bad if you don't."

"And do we?" The men, alerted by the weather forecast, had been working almost around the clock for the past two days.

Maxie sat next to Stacy and gave a satisfied nod. "They'll make it. Just. It was a good thing Rick was here to help. They're getting the last of it in the barns right now." She tapped a row of cards. "Red six on the black seven."

Stacy obediently moved the six. "As I drove this way, I saw lots of hay just sitting out in the fields in big rolls."

"Not on this ranch, you didn't. Mac built barns in the different holding areas so it can stay dry and sweet."

"Darn it, Maxie! They're all exhausted, and they're still out there working," Stacy burst out, slapping the cards on the table with frustration. "Why wouldn't they let us help?"

Maxie shrugged. "We did. We kept their fires stoked. Feeding them was as important as what they were doing. Besides, we would have been more hindrance than help out there."

"I suppose so, but—"

"I *know* so. You jockeyed that hot food out there so often, you met yourself coming and going. We did our share, and they know it. Hmm, looks like you're stuck."

"Yeah." Stacy gathered the cards, shuffled and swiftly dealt a new game. For the next few minutes, except for the snap of cards and the spit of the fire, the room was silent.

My big brother always means what he says.

Two days was long enough to fret over a statement like that, Stacy decided, neatly lining up a red nine on a black ten. More than long enough. But it wasn't a comment you'd easily forget, and each time she'd seen Mac since the day he'd flatly claimed her as his, she had wondered. And heaven only knew that she had seen plenty of him, she thought wryly. Maxie had appointed her the designated driver, and whenever she'd hauled the food out to the field in one of the pickups, Mac had been there. Oh, Lordy, had he been there—with his shirt off, muscles bunching and coiling as he moved the bales, and a sheen of sweat making him look as if he'd been oiled.

He'd always known when she was there. Each time, even over the roar of the machines when he couldn't possibly have heard her truck, he'd turned and watched her pull up. It was probably a good thing they hadn't had time to talk, she told herself bracingly, because his dark gaze had been as potent as a touch. What that man could pack into a look should be against the law, she reflected, staring blindly down at the cards.

And his touch, just a possessive brush of his lean hand against hers when he had picked up his food, had been a promise. Later, it had said.

When this is over.

Soon.

My big brother always means what he says.

The worst part was that she didn't even know if Rick had been serious. He was right about one thing, though. As well as having a positive talent for making mischief, he did have all the easy charm in the family. Stacy shook her head. *Charm,* she decided ruefully, was the last word she would use for Mac's particular blend of possessive hunger, sheer masculine determination and persistence. Intimidation, maybe, or just a tad of arrogance, but definitely not charm.

Pouncing on a black four, she moved it over to the red five. ''Odd how two men can be so alike and yet so different. In his faded jeans and scuffed boots, Rick is a carbon copy of his brother.'' Concentrating on the game, Stacy didn't realize she had spoken the thought aloud until Maxie disagreed.

"No way. Sure, they have the McClain looks and both of them were raised on the ranch, but that's the beginning and the end of it. Rick is a city boy, pure and simple. Several years ago he asked Mac to buy out part of his interest in the ranch so he could set up a fancy clothes store in Scottsdale. So Mac owns about eighty percent of the ranch, but he's the boss of it all. Rick comes to visit and help every couple of months, but after a few days he's always ready to get back to the city lights."

"And that's where I'm heading first thing tomorrow, Maxie, love. My big brother's working me to death here."

The two of them, moving lightly for such big men, walked into the circle of light around the table. Their dark heads were damp from their showers and they both wore T-shirts, faded jeans and dark socks on their feet. Rick pulled out a chair and joined the women at the table, shaking his head over the cards. Mac kneed a large cushioned chair closer and sprawled in it, his dark gaze settling on Stacy's face. A flicker of pure masculine satisfaction crossed his face.

After meeting his glance for one fleeting second—long enough to curl her toes—Stacy kept her eyes on the cards. *He knows,* she thought, panic making her fingers clumsy. Damn it, he knows.

What had she expected? she wondered gloomily. Love wasn't exactly an easy thing to hide. Concealing her feelings from Mac for another week had been a calculated risk at best. More risk than calculation, she thought with hindsight, staring at the blur of red and black before her. She had been mad, crazy as a rabid squirrel to think she could get away with it—especially when she was cursed with such a transparent face. A face she had finally schooled to keep business matters confidential but still revealed as much as Mac's hideaway pool when it came to her emotions.

"When are you going to get some comfortable furniture in here, Mac?" Rick demanded, turning the straight-backed chair around and straddling it. He reached out and slid an ace to the top.

Mac shrugged. "There's no rush. I just kept the good pieces when I redid the house. It'll take a while to find the right things."

Which means he's going to let his wife do it, Stacy decided bleakly, slapping a black seven on a black eight. "It's too bad I didn't know what you were doing out here," she said chattily, frowning at the two black cards. "I had a whole houseful of solid old pieces that would have looked wonderful in here."

Maxie turned a scandalized face toward her. "You never sold them at that big garage sale you had!"

"I was thinking about it," Stacy admitted, "but the aunts and uncles descended like a hoard of locusts and cleaned me out. They took everything but the junk."

"Girl, what you were planning to do is just short of criminal. You must have been in one big hurry to see the back of that place."

"You don't know the half of it, Maxie." Stacy frowned at the mess she had made of the hand and swept the cards together. Shuffling them, she avoided Mac's steady gaze and darted a look at Rick. "Tell me about your store," she demanded, setting the cards aside.

She should have asked him earlier, she reflected five minutes later. His enthusiastic monologue would have filled the tense silences that frequently hovered in the room when Mac was around. She learned that Rick had a very pricey men's store, and that Scottsdale was on the outskirts of Phoenix. While business was not exactly booming, it would improve because his was the only clothing store in the midst of an artists' colony. He was surrounded by art galleries, pottery shops, Indian jewelery, woven wall hangings and a hundred other arts and crafts.

"Do you sell hats?" she asked idly. She didn't particularly care, but she figured the question was good for another five minutes or so. She was wrong.

He nodded. "A few."

Her brows rose. "I'm surprised. I'd think that women would drag their men in and make them buy those sexy cowboy hats. You know, the straw kind with the brim rolled up on the sides and pulled down in front and back?"

Too late, she realized she had just described Mac's hat to a tee.

Rick gave her a surprised look. "Sexy? I'd say they're practical."

"You're not a woman," she said with an airy wave of her hand, silently cursing her quick tongue.

Maxie came to her rescue. "What do men know?" she asked the room at large. "I vote with Stacy. They may be practical, but they're also sexy."

Stacy shot a quick glance in the direction of the large chair and wished she hadn't. Mac's dark gaze was pure speculation. Ensnared by the masculine anticipation in his eyes, she stared, forgetting to breathe.

Rick cleared his throat. "How do you vote, Mac?"

"I never thought about it." He watched with interest as Stacy's cheeks got pinker. "But I have a feeling I'll think twice about wearing it in the rain."

"Yeah. It might droop. Maybe I should try to find some kind of plastic covers for them to carry in the store."

"Might be a good idea. There's dust and wind to worry about, too."

The two women exchanged patient glances. Stacy slid the cards into the pack and got up to replace them in the chest across the room. When she turned around, Rick was standing before her, waiting. She jumped, thinking he moved as quietly as his brother.

His large hands cupped her shoulders, holding her still, and he bent down to kiss one cheek, then the other. "I'll be on my way to Scottsdale by the time you get up in the morning. When I come back, I expect to see you. Hear me?"

Stacy blinked. "Then make sure you come back within a week." She didn't let her gaze stray from his face to where Mac was sitting, watching and listening. "Because as soon as my car's fixed, I'll be on my way."

He looked at her, amusement gleaming in his dark eyes. "I'll be seeing you." He gave her a final kiss on the tip of her nose and turned to his brother. "See you whenever I get back." Mac nodded, and the two of them exchanged broad grins.

"Take care," Stacy said as he headed for the door.

"I always do."

Maxie followed Rick. "I'm heading for bed, too. Good night, you two. See you in the morning."

Stacy pushed her chair close to the table, darting an oblique look at Mac. He hadn't moved. He was still sprawled in the oversize chair like a big cat. Still between her and the door. Still watching her.

And making her very, very nervous.

"Well," she said brightly, edging around him, "it's getting late. I'll—" Stacy made the mistake of looking directly at him, and the dark intent in his eyes made her forget what she was going to say. Turning on her heel, she fled from the room.

Damn the man, she thought furiously, dashing for the stairs. He'd let her go. After all those combustible glances, after sitting there looking like a man about to stake a claim, he'd simply let her walk—well, run—away.

It was just as well, she decided contrarily, flying up the stairs. She had been on the verge of doing something very foolish. If he had crooked his finger, she would have gone to him. If he had opened his arms, she would have curled up in his lap. If he had—

Well, he hadn't, she reminded herself fiercely, torn between frustration and utter relief. He hadn't said a thing about making love or whatever euphemisms men used these days to cover their basic needs.

And it was probably a good thing he hadn't, she told herself bracingly. Her two brief affairs had been with young men who were little more than tall boys. They certainly hadn't prepared her to deal with a man like Mac.

At least she hadn't made a fool of herself. She could be grateful for that. As soon as her car was ready, she would be free to go. Free as a bird, with no regrets. Leaving no complications behind.

By the time her foot touched the second-floor landing, she had convinced herself that she'd just had a very narrow escape.

"Stacy."

The stark hunger in the single word stopped her as effectively as the long arm that reached out and snagged her waist. Mac's hand covered her mouth to muffle her startled shriek. He swung her around, lightly pinning her between the oak banister and his hard body, then lifted his hand.

"Dammit, Mac," she said furiously, "I told you to quit sneaking up on me. You scared me to death." Then a gust of anger, hurt pride and adrenaline roared through her, reminding her why she had been running. Narrowing her eyes, she demanded through gritted teeth, "What...do...you...want?"

"You." He pressed closer, letting her feel his arousal, his need.

Stacy blinked. Mac's body was as bluntly honest as he was, she thought dazedly, looking up at his taut expression. He made no pretty speeches, didn't bother to soften his words. What you saw was what you got, and right now, he was as hungry as he was hot. A shiver went through her as she remembered Rick's comment. Mac did indeed mean exactly what he said. If he said he wanted her, he wanted her.

And when he'd claimed her as his?

Stacy closed her eyes, unable to deal with the ramifications of that for the moment. She was swamped by the rush of her own needs as well as his. She wanted Mac more than she had ever wanted anything in her whole life. The need to touch him and be touched was far stronger than all the questions in the world. She knew it wasn't smart, knew it wasn't the right time, knew it probably wasn't right, period. None of that mattered, though. She wanted to be close to him, to feel his naked body against hers.

And that was just for starters.

She looked up at him, too needy to be any less direct than he was. "Where?"

Mac stiffened, narrowing his eyes as he studied her face. "If you come with me, it's for the whole night," he warned softly. "There'll be no stopping this time."

Her smile was slow, small and very feminine. "Is that a promise?"

Silently Mac moved back and tugged her to his side, gesturing toward his room at the opposite end of the hall from hers.

Stacy stepped into his room, looking around as he silently closed the door behind them. It was very much like Mac, she decided. Large and masculine, with a touch of spare elegance. And it had one of the largest beds she had ever seen.

Mac wrapped his arms around her waist, pulling her back against him, sighing when she rested her head in the hollow of his shoulder, sliding her soft hands over his. "Oh, babe, you feel wonderful. I thought I was going to go crazy these last two days. I needed to hold you as much as I needed food and water."

He slid his palm over her flat stomach, fingering the purple fabric of her jumpsuit. "Nice," he murmured, nuzzling her nape. "What is it?"

Stacy shivered. "Silk," she said vaguely. "Impractical, but one of those things that women break down and spend their money on."

"Thank God." His voice held a distinctly possessive note when he added, "I hope you're not planning to wear it outside the house."

Stacy stiffened. "Why? You have a problem with that?"

"Yeah, I do." His hand dropped to cup the soft mound at the apex of her thighs. "Because I don't need a bunkhouse full of men climbing the walls. It's bad enough that I am."

"You are?" She looked over her shoulder at him with a pleased smile. "Really?"

Mac stared at her in disbelief. The crazy woman didn't have the foggiest idea what she did to him. Without a word he turned her around to face him, bringing her closer, until the gentle curves of her breasts crushed against his chest. He slid his hands down to her bottom, gently pressing her hips against his, letting her feel his fully aroused body.

"Yeah, I am."

"Oh." Gratified, Stacy rubbed her cheek against his shoulder, then jerked, stilling against him. "Mac, what? What's the matter?"

"Nothing." He swallowed heavily, taking a deep breath.

"You groaned!"

"So would you if you felt the way I do right now."

She gave a tentative wiggle. "Maybe I should move."

"No. Stay...right where you are." He patted her backside. "Relax." He stroked her, his fingers kneading a trail down her spine, over the lush curve of her bottom and the back of her thigh.

He slowed down, trying to think with his head instead of his groin. This was a lady who had some definite doubts about her sex appeal. She had looked at him as if he had been trying to sell her swampland when he told her she was beautiful. He would take it easy.

Damned easy, because she was as skittish as a virgin.

Mac blinked, staring thoughtfully at the top of her head, feeling like he had just been hit by a freight train. Virgin? Was there a twenty-seven-year-old woman left in the country who was still a virgin? he wondered, automatically tightening his grip.

Maybe.

And if there was, she just might be clinging to him, wondering what the hell she was doing there.

"Stacy?"

"Um?"

"You're not going to say no tonight, are you?" It was her last chance, he told himself. One more than he wanted to give her, but maybe just the one she needed.

This time he was ready when she jumped. He curved his fingers around her nape, brushing his thumb through her hair. She was as tense as a cat poised to pounce—or run away.

She shook her head and took a ragged breath. "I thought we settled that out in the hall. No."

"No what?" he persisted, wanting to be certain they were talking about the same thing.

"No, I'm not going to say no!" She bit the words off in exasperation.

Mac soothed her with his hands, waiting until she began to melt into him; then he said, "Honey?"

Stacy stopped breathing, tensing again. "What?"

"Are you on the pill?"

After a pause that was just a bit too long, she slowly shook her head. "No. There, uh, hasn't been any reason for a while."

Mac tightened his grip on her. "How long is a while?" he asked cautiously.

"Good grief! Does it really matter?" She looked up at him, her face as heated as her words.

"Yeah," he drawled, holding her still. "It does. If you're going to get the pleasure out of this that you deserve to have. That I want you to have." He shook her lightly. "Just give me a damn number and get it over with."

Stacy buried her face in his neck. "This is embarrassing," she mumbled.

Mac squeezed her bottom. "A number," he said patiently.

"Four."

"Four months?"

Her sigh was a warm puff against his neck. "Years."

"Four years," he said blankly, certain he had misunderstood. When she didn't say anything, he repeated, "Four *years?* Where the hell were you, in a damn convent?"

"That's enough!" In an instant she was all sharp elbows and knees, trying to get away from him. "I didn't know I was going to have to fill out a blasted questionnaire. I think I've been embarrassed enough. Let's just forget I ever came in here, okay?"

Mac held her, one arm slanted from her shoulder to her waist, the other across her bottom, keeping her where she was. "Just hold on a minute," he murmured soothingly, repeating the words while she struggled, waiting for her to calm down. "It's okay, honey, everything's all right."

It took a while. Finally she took a shuddering breath and stilled. Gradually, one by one, her muscles relaxed as she slumped against him.

"I'd rather have you embarrassed than hurt," he said evenly, turning her face up and covering her mouth with a swift kiss. He held her there, glorying in the feel of her soft body against his, deepening the kiss, groaning her name against her lips when her fingertips languidly began to stroke through his hair.

When her hands dropped to his shoulders, her nails sinking into the fabric of his shirt, Mac raised his head and took a ragged breath. Her dazed expression filled him with fierce satisfaction that almost equaled his hunger.

She wanted him, he thought exultantly. She was on fire. For *him*. Intoxicated with the knowledge, he wanted to strut like a peacock, build a fence around her and hang a sign on it telling the world that she was his.

Instead, he kissed her. "You're so soft, sweetheart. I want to feel you against me. Not silk, just you."

Stacy blinked, jolted by the urgency in his muttered words. Mac's honesty was overwhelming. Exciting. She felt the same way. She wanted to touch him, to feel his sleek body unhampered by clothes.

Nodding, she fumbled with the gold belt at her waist, dropping it to the floor. While she lowered the front zipper of the jumpsuit, hearing the rasp of metal teeth loud in the silent room, Mac tore off his clothes and tossed them aside.

"Oh, Mac." Stacy forgot what she was doing. Bare to the waist except for a wispy bra, the purple fabric clinging to her hips, she ran an exploring hand down Mac's chest. His white cotton briefs were a stark contrast to his bronzed body and did nothing to conceal his arousal. "You're beautiful."

"Don't stop now, babe." He clamped his hand over hers, holding it still, waiting.

Her green eyes filled with sudden anticipation, Stacy impatiently shimmied out of the jumpsuit and kicked it aside. While it was still in midair, she flung herself at Mac.

With a triumphant sound that fell somewhere between a growl and a laugh, he scooped her up and tossed her gently onto the big bed, following her down and holding her close. He rolled aside long enough to dispose of her lacy bra and panties, then pulled her back against him.

Stacy braced a hand against his chest, stopping him. Sliding her hand down, her thumb hooking beneath the elastic band of his briefs, she looked up, blinking at the anticipation in his dark eyes. "Take them off," she muttered impatiently.

Mac's teasing grin was a slash of white. "I took yours off," he pointed out in a reasonable tone. "It's your turn."

Sudden speculation gleaming in her eyes, Stacy scrambled to her knees, lured by Mac's teasing chuckle. No one had told her this could be fun, she thought, grazing his stomach with her hand, her lips curving in a small, feminine smile at his indrawn breath.

When Mac lifted his hips, he knew he had made a big mistake. She took her time skimming the briefs down, brushing his thighs with her breasts, sliding her small, soft hands down his loins, hesitating for a heart-stopping second, then moving down his thighs and legs.

There was no way in hell he could take this slowly enough for her if she kept flowing over him like warm honey. Four years, he reminded himself deliberately. For her, it was almost like the first time, and he had to take it slowly. He groaned when she ran her fingers back up his thighs.

Slowly, he thought grimly. If she'd let him.

Mac hauled her back up, tucking her head against his arm and leaned over her.

Stacy blinked at him uncertainly. "Don't you want me to touch you?"

"Oh, babe, yeah," he said hoarsely. "Later. You can do any damn thing you want. Later." He lowered his head, his hand locked in her hair, brushing kisses along the line of her jaw, dropping to the curve of her throat, murmuring encouragement when she shivered. Stacy slid her arms around his neck, nestling closer, turning her face into his throat, touching him first with her lips, then her tongue. His groan rewarded her, and she laced her fingers in his thick hair, framing his head, tugging him closer.

"That's it, honey, hold me. Tighter."

Mac covered her mouth with his, deepening the kiss, touching her tongue with his. He felt the jolt through her body when he cupped her breast and stroked the beaded nipple with his thumb.

"Mac?"

He smiled at the breathless gasp. "Yeah, it's me." When the restless movement of her legs brought them against his, he tensed. Four years, he reminded himself again. All that passion had been locked away. So if it killed him—and it just might—he was not going to rush her. This one was for her. And after tonight he would be imprinted on her—body and soul. After tonight she wouldn't be able to look at another man, much less touch one.

Stacy cried out when he touched the tip of his tongue to her breast.

"Mac!"

He shuddered at the wild cry, holding her closer. She was like a stick of dynamite, he thought, awed. And he was the match. Any second now—just one more touch— and she was going to blow sky-high, taking him right along with her.

Stacy clutched at his shoulders. "I want you."

"Good." He pressed his lips on the wild pulse in her throat, running his hand over her rib cage, touching, testing every inch of her silky skin, feeling the excitement shimmering through her, reacting to her incredible response as if she had stroked him with her soft hands.

"Mac, *do* something! Help me. I ache!"

He kissed her flushed face and shook his head. "Aching isn't enough," he told her, dropping a hard kiss on her mouth. "I want you going crazy. I want your legs wrapped around me, holding me and never letting go."

When his fingers brushed the soft triangle of hair above her thighs, Stacy gasped. "No more, Mac. I mean it, no more!" She pressed her legs together, but Mac's questing hand was sliding down again, offering her pleasure she'd never before had. Curiosity and excitement battled with a primitive, feminine uncertainty, and, barely aware of his husky encouragement, she parted her legs, giving him access.

Mac accepted the invitation, reaching for the small nub of femininity. At the first touch, Stacy gasped and clutched at him. Shivers of tension and electric excitement flooded through her. Tiny convulsions shook her body and she cried out again, arching her back.

"Mac!"

Exultant, knowing he had brought her satisfaction, he flowed over her, into her, held there by her arms and legs, drawn deeper by the last of the convulsions tightening her body.

"Stacy!" He shuddered in her arms, the sound of her name blending with the small sighs of satisfaction she made deep in her throat. All of them were his name.

Mac went still in her arms, on top of her, never wanting to move again.

Several minutes later he opened his eyes and brushed her shoulder with his lips. "I'm probably crushing you," he muttered, rolling to his back, taking her with him. "Stacy?" He cupped her bottom, squeezing a little. "Are you okay?"

She nodded, rubbing her cheek against his chest. "Are you?"

"Lady, I have never been so okay in my life."

"Me, neither." She propped her arms on his chest, rested her chin on her wrists and looked down at him with an earnest expression. "I didn't know it could be like that," she confided.

Mac grinned. "As a matter of fact, neither did I." His smile broadened at her blink of surprise. Now what? he wondered, watching her expressive face. She had the disconcerted look of a woman who had suddenly realized that she was sprawled naked on top of a man and was now wondering how to get herself safely under the covers.

He was right.

"Uh, Mac?"

"Yeah?"

She braced her arms on his chest and levered herself up several inches. High enough to give him an entrancing view of her breasts. "Am I too heavy? Should I move?" she added hopefully.

He grinned again. "Don't even think of it. You're just fine." He threaded his fingers through her silky hair and drew her face closer, close enough to brush his lips across hers. "You're perfect. Think of me as a mattress," he suggested, sliding her legs down on his. "I want to feel every inch of you."

"You might want to go to sleep," she suggested reasonably. "This can't be comfortable for you."

Mac clasped his hands over her bottom, keeping her hips pressed against his. "We've got a long night ahead of us," he murmured, "and I'm not planning on doing much sleeping."

Eight

"Stacy? Ready for some breakfast?" Maxie elbowed the door open and dropped a large wicker tray on Mac's dresser.

"Maxie!" Stacy bolted upright in bed, clutching the sheet to her breasts, staring aghast at the other woman. She didn't need a mirror to know what Maxie's blue eyes were seeing. She was a mess, she thought with a groan, a wide-eyed, pink-cheeked, rumpled picture of guilt. Add well-kissed lips and whisker burns to the picture, and you had one definitely not designed for a second cousin twice removed.

After taking a hasty glance around the room, she wished she hadn't. Her jumpsuit was a wrinkled pool of purple silk in the middle of the creamy beige carpet. Her panties dangled from the arm of Mac's chair, and her bra was— She groaned again, not seeing it. God only knew where her bra was.

"No need to be embarrassed, kiddo." Maxie picked up her clothes and considerately put them at the foot of the bed. "There aren't any secrets in this house. As big as the place is, it's too small for that."

Stacy narrowed her eyes. "Did Mac—"

"Say anything about this?" Maxie gave her a you-should-know-better-than-that look and shook her head. "Not a word."

"Then how—"

"Did I know?" She lifted the tray, took another look at Stacy hugging the sheet, sighed and put the tray back down. She pulled one of Mac's shirts out of the closet and dropped it in Stacy's lap. "Here. Get into this and scoot back against the headboard." Turning her back, she said, "How did I know? Because ever since you came, I've watched Mac getting tighter than a drawn bow. He was like a stick of dynamite ready to go off. Are you decent?"

Stacy sighed. "Yes."

Maxie settled the tray over Stacy's legs, poured two cups of coffee and gestured at a plate of French toast. "Dig in." She waited until Stacy lifted the fork, then pulled up a chair and settled in for a cozy chat.

"So," she continued after a swallow of coffee, "this morning he came down to breakfast looking five years younger. If he had been a fiddle, his strings would have been sagging. If he was a hunk of ice, he'd have been a puddle. If he was—"

"I get the picture," Stacy said hastily. And she did. She knew exactly what Maxie meant. After all, hadn't she spent the last nine hours with the man?

"And then," Maxie concluded with a grin, "he said in this offhanded voice men use when they think they're putting something over on you, that you were probably tired after all that cooking and, more than likely, you'd be down late. Men," she snorted. "They're about as subtle as a sledgehammer."

Stacy finished her breakfast and placed her fork on the plate, eyeing the other woman warily. Maxie had fallen into silent communion with her coffee mug, and Stacy realized that a reticent Maxie made her distinctly edgy. She had a nasty feeling that any second the other shoe was about to fall.

Maxie put her mug on the tray and tilted her head, studying Stacy's face. "So?" she finally asked.

Stacy took a fortifying swallow of coffee. "I'm not sure I know what you're asking me," she said cautiously.

Maxie gave another snort. "Well, I'm sure not asking how my cousin is in bed."

"Second cousin," Stacy said absently, wondering what was coming next. After all the time she had spent with Maxie, the only thing she was completely certain of was that Maxie was totally unpredictable.

"Twice removed," Maxie agreed. "What I want to know is, are you going to move in here with Mac?"

"Here?" Stacy looked around. "I'm already here. I'm staying in his house, remember?"

"Lord love a duck," Maxie sighed. "Some people are dense. I mean *here,*" she emphasized, pointing first to the floor, then the bed. "In his room."

"Oh." Stacy flushed. "I hadn't thought about it."

"Well, think. Now."

"I don't know, Maxie," she hedged. "Mac didn't suggest it, and he might think I was taking a lot for granted if I just moved in." A *whole* lot, she thought cravenly. It was one thing to sleep with a woman, entirely another to find that she's taken half of your closet, your dresser and your bed.

"No, he wouldn't."

"He might need a lot of personal space," she said desperately.

Maxie made an exasperated noise that sounded like *tchaw*. "That sounds like one of those weird California notions. There's enough space in this room for a whole family."

"The bottom line," Stacy said flatly, "is that he might not *want* me here. And I don't want to embarrass either one of us."

Maxie stared at her. "Are we talking about the same man? Mac? Girl, have you seen the look on his face when he watches you? I can't think of anything he'd like more than walking in here after a hard day and seeing your things scattered around the room."

Stacy twisted her napkin, thinking she would like it, too. Too much. But it was a dangerous idea, one that suggested permanence, or at least more time than she had.

"Maxie," she said gently, "you know I'm leaving in a few days. I don't think it would be a good idea."

"I know you *say* you're going," Maxie said bluntly. "I also know that Mac will do everything he can to change your mind." She shrugged. "Anyway, why not make the most of the time you have? Why put yourself to the trouble of tromping up and down that long hall? But before you make up your mind, think about this. All you've talked about is what you think Mac does or doesn't want. Maybe you ought to think about what *you* want."

She got to her feet and took the tray. "There's no one in the house, so it's safe to wear Mac's shirt when you go back to your room." Tucking the tray under one arm, she opened the door. Looking back over her shoulder, she said, "Stacy, you've been real honest about your plans, but I hope you think long and hard before you take off. I think you could be happy here, and I've never seen Mac look the way he did this morning. Don't break his heart, okay?"

For the next couple of hours, Stacy deliberately avoided thinking about Maxie's suggestion. First things first, she decided, taking stock of her various aches and twinges, some in the most surprising places. Mac had been right about one thing, she reflected wryly, grinning at the thought. Neither of them had slept much.

She took a hot, leisurely bath in her room, enjoying the voluptuous lap of water on her body. Her sigh was one of sheer pleasure, reminding her of the times she had sighed during the night, pulsing with pleasure, calling out to Mac. She had done things her alter ego, the staid Ms. Sullivan, had never even heard of, she thought with wicked satisfaction.

She had made love with a man she loved. She had touched and been touched in ways she had never dreamed of. Oddly enough, Mac seemed to think that he had found in her, Stacy Sullivan, the perfect match for his staggering sensuality. She blinked thoughtfully at the novel idea, then grinned.

Maybe he had.

She didn't have to be an experienced lover to know that he was, but apparently he was even more than that. He was a perceptive man who had taken one look and seen in her a wellspring of potential.

She had always been a fast learner, she reminded herself, with a small smile. Her intellect had never been in question, nor had her instincts. Unfortunately, until now, all of her energies since college had been devoted to business.

No, the key word here was *fortunately,* she decided, scooping up some of the scented bubbles and lathering them on her arms. The discoveries she had made last night were all the more exciting and precious for having been made in Mac's arms.

In Mac's bed.

On Mac's floor.

In Mac's bathtub.

During a storm where thunder came in deafening rolls and jagged fingers of lightning illuminated their bed.

Yes, fortunate, because he had been more than hungry, tender, demanding and highly inventive, she reflected, stepping out of the tub. He had also been protective, placing a box of condoms on the bedside table—and using them.

She slipped into shorts and a matching shirt—lime green—and gazed around the room that had been hers for the last few days, Maxie's question nagging at her. It was time to quit stalling and make a decision.

She knew it wasn't merely a matter of whether or not she would hang her clothes in Mac's closet and sleep in his bed. That would simply be the result of another decision.

No, the issue was larger than that. It had to do with Prudence, her life there, the woman she had become and the woman she dreamed of being. The reason she had left in the first place.

Leaving Prudence had taken more courage than anything she had ever done. Staying all those years had not been an act of bravery, it had been her only choice. Even when she had sold the company at a satisfying profit, it would have been far easier to stay and be Ms. Sullivan than to drive across the country looking for a special place and the woman she hoped to become.

It had been a gamble hinged on a dream—the known past against an uncertain future. And did she have any regrets?

No. Absolutely not. She had lived more in the past three weeks on the road than she had in the last four years in Prudence.

But now she was facing another step in the unfolding of Stacy Sullivan—and a harder decision than the first one because it involved someone else. Trusting someone else. Did she reach out with both hands and take the man she wanted, the loving she wanted? Did she take the risk, knowing it was only temporary?

Stacy took a deep breath, knowing she was stalling, knowing the decision was already made.

Yes, dammit, she did!

She reached up and swept the hangers off the clothes pole and marched down the hall to Mac's room.

Mac stepped off the path onto the boulder, the first in the series of steps. The need to be near Stacy had magnified with each passing hour, and now instinct had brought him here. His eyes narrowed in satisfaction when he saw the quilt that Maxie insisted Stacy bring to sit on.

She was here.

Spending last night with her hadn't eased the ache. If anything, now that he knew the strength and softness of her slim body, and had soared with her reckless spirit, it was worse. Feeling her sheathe him and urge him even closer had been a pleasure that neared pain. He had never wanted a woman like that, had never been wanted like that. And now he wanted more.

One night, spectacular as it had been, didn't even make a dent in his need for her. Another night, a week, a month—hell, ten years—wouldn't do it, either. Maybe a lifetime. It would at least be a start.

He stepped over the quilt, noted that it was draped over a basket and leapt to the second boulder. There were nine of them in all, circling around at an angle, culminating in a natural pool. He had spent a lot of hot summer days in the pool and was gambling that the cool water held the same attraction for Stacy. He climbed quietly, even though he knew that the bubbling water would cover any sounds he made. He had an unexpected urge to see Stacy before she spotted him, wanted to watch her dreaming in his private place.

When his eyes were level with the last boulder, Mac stopped, his brows lifting. He was going to see more of Stacy than he'd bargained for, he thought with a grin as he studied a tumble of green and peach fabric.

Silently he climbed the rest of the way and leaned against a lip of the last rock, next to her straw hat. Since the pool was less than four feet away, Mac had an unimpeded view.

She was as playful as a water sprite, half-turned away from him, cupping the water in her hands and tossing it into the air, blinking as the iridescent drops rode on the slight breeze and sprayed down on her.

The water came to just below her breasts, but it was so clear she could have been standing behind glass. It was also cool enough to shape her nipples into taut, mauve beads. So much for watching Stacy dream, Mac thought ruefully, his eyes narrowing as hunger roared through him, tightening his loins. He reached over to pick up a pebble and tossed it in the water.

When it landed less than six inches in front of her, Stacy whirled with a startled shriek, crossing her arms in front of her.

"Too late, sweetheart," he drawled. "I've seen it already. All of it." He grinned. "And it's mighty pretty, wet or dry."

"Mac! You scared the daylights out of me," she gasped. "I swear, I'm going to hang a bell on you."

He grinned again. He couldn't help it. She was all round green eyes, pink cheeks and perky nipples. She was also trying to back away, but since there was no place to go, she just gave him a better view by pressing her pretty bottom against the far side of the pool.

"I told you you're safe up here," he said mildly, pulling off one of his boots and reaching for the other. "No reason to get excited."

"You, uh, didn't call out this time," she said in a flustered tone. "You surprised me."

"I was alone. There was no reason to call." He unbuttoned his shirt and took it off, tossing it next to her clothes before moving closer to her.

"Mac, what are you doing?" Alarm tightened her voice.

He looked down at his bare feet, then back at her. "Taking my clothes off."

She closed her eyes briefly in exasperation. "I can see that. Why?"

He grinned and slowly unbuttoned his jeans. "Because I'm hot and the water's cool."

"Is that the only reason?" she asked huskily, touching her upper lip with her tip of her tongue.

"No." He stood there, waiting, his dark eyes taking in every emotion on her expressive face. He didn't realize he had been holding his breath until she began to smile; then he exhaled sharply and hooked his thumbs beneath his waistband, pushing down his jeans and briefs at the same time. He kicked them off and stood there, as naked as she was, giving her time to get used to him. Again.

Stacy blinked. They had been too close last night, too driven, too anxious to touch, to be touched. This was her first opportunity to actually study him, all of him. Her fingers had touched every square inch of him, but now she intended to take all the time she wanted just to look.

Mac was magnificent.

Incredibly wide shoulders and muscular arms were the result of a lifetime of hard work, but she knew they could offer shelter with a tenderness that equaled the strength. His chest was massive, ridged with muscles and a dark triangle of hair that narrowed and trailed down his stomach. Her eyes followed the dark, silky trail to a denser thatch of hair and stopped abruptly.

"Good heavens," she said faintly.

Mac threw back his head and gave a roar of laughter. Easing into the water, he reached for her, still chuckling, but his amusement faded abruptly when Stacy flung herself at him in a rush of spray, her taut nipples nudging his chest. She made a purring sound against his shoulder and stood on her toes to slide her arms around his neck.

"Is that the only reason you came?" she murmured again. "To cool off?"

His arms tightened around her. "No." The single word was blunt with need. "Because I'm starved."

"Ah. Well, this is your lucky day." She gave him a brilliant smile, her eyes alight with mischief. "It just so happens that Maxie packed me an enormous lunch, with an incredible variety of things in it."

"The food is just a bonus," Mac said tightly, clamping his hands around her slender waist and holding her so there was just one source of contact. When he lifted her slowly, deliberately, her nipples traced an electric trail up his chest.

"Oh, Mac," Stacy said, closing her eyes. "I don't know what you do to me."

"Whatever it is, it's pretty basic." He hauled her against him, letting her feel the extent of his arousal. "It's also mutual. Wrap your legs around me, honey. Get closer."

She shifted, her thighs tightening around his waist, her arms looped around his neck, her hands clenching in his thick hair. Basic, he'd said, she thought hazily. Oh, my, yes, it was that, all right. Mac was sensual, caring, lusty, and she gloried in the fact that she was woman to his man, a mate, matching his needs, responding in full measure to his caresses.

Back in Prudence she had watched friends her own age involved in the inevitable mating games, envying the women who glowed with love, wondering if she would ever find a man who made her soul sing with excitement, her body shudder with response. And now that she had, she knew it was far more wonderful than she had imagined.

She lifted her face, smiling when his lips brushed her lashes and skimmed down her cheeks. His hands cupped her buttocks, supporting her, and she pressed closer, until her breasts flattened against his hard chest. It still wasn't close enough, she thought, shifting impatiently, tightening her arms around his neck, feeling the hunger build within her.

It had been like that last night. Each time. The need to look, to touch, to be closer, to burn, to feel the hunger build was overwhelming. The wild excitement, his hard hands and even harder body over her, around her, in her, filling her with a glorious tension until she shattered was almost unbearable.

Then it began all over again.

Stacy's smile was small and intensely feminine. In less than twenty-four hours he had sensitized her to his touch, taught her to burn at just a thought, a glance or the sound of his voice.

And it was entirely mutual. She wanted him with the same urgency he felt for her. She had wondered all those years what it would be like, and now that she knew, she couldn't wait.

"Damn!"

Stacy opened her eyes at Mac's soft curse. "What?" she asked groggily, drowning in sensuality.

He swore again. "I forgot to bring something with me."

Snuggling closer, she murmured, "What else could we possibly need?"

He ran his hands along her thighs in an apologetic gesture. "Guess."

"Oh." She blinked up at him, her green eyes still hazy with need. "I suppose we really have to have—"

"Yeah. We do. I won't take any risks with you." He heaved a frustrated sigh and tightened his fingers on her thighs. "Slide down, sweetheart, we both need to cool off."

When her feet were once more touching the ground and she was away from the heat of his big body, Stacy shivered.

"Are you cold?"

She nodded, speechless, her body still adjusting to the sudden change.

"Then let's get out." The water made a soft, rushing sound when Mac braced his arms on the side of the pool and effortlessly surged up and out. He turned around and held out his hands, waiting. When Stacy reached out to him, he hauled her up beside him.

She shivered again, her gaze meeting his and darting away. "I should have brought something to dry off with," she blurted, not really aware of what she was saying, simply needing to fill the tense silence.

"I'll be your towel." His tone was guttural.

Before she grasped the meaning of his words, Mac's big hands brushed down her arms, then her back, smoothing away the rivulets of water trickling down her body. She shuddered when his fingers trailed down her collarbone and around her breasts, his thumbs grazing two iridescent drops clinging to her puckered nipples. But it was when his hands followed the curve of her waist to her hips, hesitating at the small triangle of hair above her thighs that she broke.

Her wild cry stunned her even more than it did Mac. It was a bereft sound, full of longing and need. Mac hauled her back into his arms for a swift, hard kiss and a muttered apology in her hair. Deliberately changing the mood, he backed up, gave her a teasing pat on her bare bottom and grinned.

"You *did* mention food, didn't you?"

Stacy nodded, not fooled for a second. His body told her in a pure, basic language that he was just as frus-

trated as she was. Nodding, she tried to match his tone.
"I think you'll be surprised at Maxie's idea of a picnic
lunch."

"Lead me to it," he ordered, calmly collecting their
clothes and bundling them under his arm. He stepped
down to the next boulder and, turning, held his free
hand out to her.

Stacy stared at him, knowing her color was rising. She
held out her hand and waggled her fingers, considering
her own perversity. When she was in Mac's arms, all she
wanted to do was tear away the clothing that separated
them—his or hers, it didn't matter. When she wasn't, her
small-town, conservative training reared its head.

"I'm not running around here in the natural," she
told him, knowing the prickling of her skin wasn't
caused by the sun. "Will you please put something on,
for heaven's sake? And give me my clothes!"

Mac grinned and tossed her the bundle he held. While
she pulled on her shorts and top, he slid into his jeans.
"Now can we get some food?" When Stacy nodded, he
took her hand and led the way down.

He spread the quilt on the flat rock while Stacy, humming, busied herself with the contents of the basket.
"Almost ready?" she asked. When she turned, Mac was
stretched out on the blanket, eyes closed, his face turned
to the sun.

She sat cross-legged beside him, the air in her lungs
backing up when she looked at him. He should have
looked relaxed, but there was an aura of savagely restrained tension in him that she might not have recog-
nized if she weren't feeling it herself. He was as fully
aroused as he had been at the pool.

"Mac?"

"Yeah?"

"I thought you were hungry."

He opened his eyes and turned toward her, propping his head on his palm. His gaze flicked from the anticipation in her green eyes to the plate she placed on the blanket beside him.

It contained several small foil packets.

His large hand wrapped around her nape and he tugged, tumbling her across his chest. "You're right," he told her, smoothing a hand down her back and sounding sinfully satisfied. "Maxie packs one hell of a lunch."

Nine

"Hey, Tumbleweed! Got a minute?"

Mac's black scowl slowed Slim down for about two seconds.

"Sorry, boss, didn't mean to yell in your ear. I just want to catch Tumbleweed before she takes off. Be right back." He dropped his hammer next to the small shed they were building behind the barn and loped across the yard.

Mac didn't ask himself why he wanted to punch someone every time one of the men chased Stacy down to talk to her. He didn't ask himself why he stiffened with temper when one of them called her by her CB handle.

He didn't bother because he knew.

Because he wanted to be the only man she turned to with a smile, the only one who made her eyes light with laughter, the only one she reached out and touched.

Even if the touch was simply a fleeting gesture of appreciation, he wanted it. Mac swore in disgust, watching as Slim waved his arms in a southerly direction, because he knew that what he *really* wanted to do was to lock her up somewhere. In a place where he'd know she was waiting at the end of every day.

For him.

And he hated that damned handle of hers more every time he heard it. He was even smart enough to figure out why.

It was a symbol of her restlessness, her freedom.

Of course he believed in freedom as much as the next person. Probably more than some, he decided, pounding a nail in a two-by-four with one savage swing of his hammer. But there was something wrong with the idea, if it meant that a woman who knew squat about the rough side of life could take off whenever she wanted and end up rubbing elbows with big-city scum.

Of course, there were decent people out there, too, he reminded himself, taking another nail out of the canvas tool bag tied at his waist. But they weren't the ones he worried about. It just made sense that when someone was so naive she believed she could test the ground for power spots and looked for help in books about meditating and finding herself, she was just naturally going to gravitate toward trouble.

He slammed another nail into the frame and decided that naive wasn't exactly the word. Lots of people had strange reading habits these days. It didn't take a genius to figure that out; all you had to do was walk into a bookstore and look at the stuff people were buying.

Unworldly was the word he was looking for, he decided, whamming another nail. He had a hunch that living in a town named Prudence, somewhere in Kansas, population less than five thousand, didn't exactly prepare people to live on the cutting edge. He could see that it might give them a strong itch to try it, but their actual, practical experience would be diddly-squat.

Especially someone like Stacy. In spite of his grim mood, he grinned. He could just imagine her in that label factory, flitting like a butterfly from job to job, leaving a long line of relieved supervisors behind her. Not because she couldn't do the job, he knew. The lively intelligence in her green eyes was proof of that. No, he imagined it had more to do with her restless spirit, curiosity and her determined crusade for more—more adventure, more excitement, more of everything.

He could no more imagine her working on an assembly line than he could picture Maxie knitting baby bootees. Actually, his imagination boggled at the thought of Stacy doing anything that became routine. He could picture her in college, driving a conscientious counselor mad as she dabbled in art and self-defense classes.

If she ever harnessed all that energy, he reflected, she'd be formidable, in whatever she aimed for. Again he thought of the startling intelligence in her eyes and wondered why her family had allowed her to run hogwild. They had done her no favor, that was for sure. All she needed was a little discipline in her life, a purpose, some sense of responsibility.

More questions, he thought in disgust, narrowly missing his thumb with the hammer. Someday they were going to have a long, serious discussion, and he was going to get some answers. Someday. When their fires weren't burning so high. When they weren't so hot to touch and be touched that they could hardly wait to get the bedroom door closed behind them.

She had moved into his room three days ago, the day they'd had the picnic by the pool—the one where Maxie's bonus pack had taken care of the first course. He shook his head, remembering how Stacy had walked to his room with him when they'd returned to the house. She had wanted to see his reaction when he first realized her things were with his.

As soon as he had opened the door, he'd known something was different, and hope had rampaged through him like wildfire. As far as he could tell, Stacy used no perfume, yet he had instantly noticed her soft, feminine scent. Her books—the three famous how-to's—rested on his desk. He had been so anxious to get to his closet, hoping to find exactly what he *did* find, that he almost tripped over his own feet.

Well, she had seen his reaction, all right. It had been pure Neanderthal and had shocked her right out of those ridiculous sandals she wore. Relief had poured through him with a rush of adrenaline. He hadn't had to ask or coax. She had come to him. She was his. Possession, pure and simple, had roared through him, and she had ended up on his bed, flat on her back, naked as he was.

It hadn't dawned on him until much later that she'd been nervous, had half expected to be tossed out of the room. Her eyes had been worried and her expressive face was geared for rejection.

More questions, he thought in aggravation. How in God's name had she ever thought he would turn her away? Didn't she have any idea what she did to a man? To him? What kind of men had she known? And why the hell hadn't she known any in the past four years? When his body tightened at the thought, he smiled grimly, knowing he'd rather be curious than eaten up with jealous rage because she *had* been.

"Sorry, boss." Slim picked up the hammer and grabbed a handful of nails. "Doc wanted me to tell Tumbleweed about this place close to the main gate."

"What about it?"

Slim shrugged and pounded industriously with the hammer.

"I said, what about it?"

"Hey, it's nothing to get steamed up about. Doc just thought she might be interested, that's all."

"In *what?*"

Slim eyed the nails as if they were his ticket to salvation. "Well, it was the place where he had that fight with Gil, from Elwood Vance's spread. Remember? Tall guy that outweighed him by about fifty pounds? When they started, Doc thought he was a goner, but he ended up pounding old Gil into the ground. Remember that?"

"I remember."

Slim winced at Mac's biting tone. "Well, anyway, Doc started thinking about what Tumbleweed's looking for, and he thought she might like to take a look. He's real fond of that spot these days."

Mac swore. "And how about the rest of you? I suppose you're all sending her on the same kind of idiotic chase?"

Slim flushed. "Well, hell, boss, she asks. She wants to know."

"So? Are you?"

"Andy just told her about the place he fought off that cougar, and Mick showed her where he stepped into a nest of rattlers and got off without a bite."

"Any others?"

"Well, yeah. I guess we've all mentioned one place or another. You know how it is. We're just trying to help."

"By making the place sound like a disaster area. Don't be so damned helpful from now on, okay?"

Slim grabbed another nail and started pounding, recognizing an order when he heard one. "Anything you say, boss. Anything you say."

* * *

"What's that in your hand?"

Stacy looked up at Mac from where she sat on the gently swaying porch swing. Her smile was so dreamily seductive, that his body tightened, and he wondered if the lady from Prudence had ever made love on a porch swing.

She patted the seat beside her. "Do you have time to sit for a while?

"I'm the boss, remember?" He sat next to her, his weight propelling the swing off at an oblique tangent. As it calmed down, he scooped her up and settled her across his thighs, dropping a quick kiss at the corner of her mouth. "I can take a break whenever I want."

"Sure," she agreed, nuzzling her cheek against his shoulder. "As long as a mare doesn't decide she's going to have a baby—"

"Foal."

"Foal," she echoed. "And as long as a stallion doesn't kick down a fence to get to some unsuspecting female, your time is your own."

"Damn straight, lady." He slid his arm around her, skimming her rib cage and the underside of her breasts, wondering how long they would last this time. When he was near her, he had to touch her. It was as simple and vital as that. When he did, she was so soft and silky that his hands shook and his heart pounded. When she sighed and softened against him as she was doing now, he burned, ready to toss her over his shoulder and haul her upstairs.

"What do you have in your hand?" he repeated, cupping her hand in his bigger one, trying to ignore the way her hip pressed against him, massaging him as the swing drifted back and forth. He wondered if the time would ever come when he could have a lengthy conversation with her, actually talk for a reasonable period of time, before he picked her up and headed for someplace private where he could take off her clothes.

He might have made it before this if Stacy had put up any resistance. Any at all. But she seemed to be drowning in sensuality, responding to his touch the same way he did to hers. No, he reflected, looking into green eyes shining with invitation and anticipation, this was not the way for a man to keep his mind on a conversation.

Mac squeezed her hand, and she slowly uncurled her fingers, revealing several of the polished rocks she had picked up from the pool area. She was like a kid in a candy store when she went there, he thought, recalling how she patiently sifted through the sand and gravel, exclaiming with pleasure when she found one just the right size or color. She had almost filled a small basket Maxie had given her with them.

Although Stacy maintained she liked them simply because they were pretty, Mac was convinced that they appealed to her because of their sensual nature. Each one was polished to a gloss and as smooth as a marble. When she sifted her fingers through them, she looked as if she were being stroked by silk.

"You carry these around with you?" he asked, prodding one of them with the tip of his finger.

Stacy nodded. "They remind me of the grotto."

"That's an awful fancy word for some rocks and water," he teased.

"Grotto," she repeated firmly, giving him a severe frown. "You make it sound like a mud puddle. It's more than that, and you know it. It has sheltering trees, leaves whispering in the breeze, clear springwater that sounds like babies laughing, stones gleaming like gold—"

Mac bent his head and kissed away the frown, pleased that she was defending it with such energy. "All right, you win. We'll call it whatever you want—the spring, the pool, the grotto, whatever."

"Then it's settled," she said in a satisfied voice. "The grotto. Our place."

He mulled that over, hearing again the contentment in her voice when she said *our place*, and he knew that he could spend the rest of his life doing just what he was doing now—holding the lady from Prudence in his arms, listening to her talk about *our place*.

"Mac?" She nudged her shoulder against his chest. "Look over there, at the dark clouds rolling in. I don't know where I got the idea that Arizona was all desert, but wherever it was, it was wrong. I've seen more rain since I've been here than I saw my last three months in Kansas."

"That's because you're in the northwestern part of the state, and up here it's monsoon season."

"I thought they had those on tropical islands."

"They do. But that's what our summer storms are called, and every July and August, regular as clockwork, they come charging in."

"They're exciting, aren't they?"

"Yeah. Especially if you're out working in them. There's nothing like dodging lightning to get your blood stirred up."

"Mac?"

His blood started pounding at the sound of her voice. It was soft, teasing and full of promise.

"Yeah?"

"Do you know something I've never done?"

Even though he shifted cautiously, moving didn't help because Stacy was on his lap, pressing against him. "Is this something on your famous list?'' he asked, easing her down on his thighs.

She shook her head. ''Well, no, not really. That's more of a collection of long-term goals. I only thought about this yesterday morning, and I was sort of hoping I wouldn't have to add it to the list.''

''Okay, I'll bite. What is it that you've never done?''

She took a shaky breath, hesitated, then said in a rush, ''I've never made love with you on a lazy afternoon in the middle of a thunderstorm.''

Mac shuddered with arousal at her words. His first impulse was to lunge off the swing and take her upstairs to get a head start on the storm. He listened to the second impulse, the one that told him to stay where he was.

In the past three days, he had been lucky to remember that he had a ranch. All he could think about was Stacy. Stacy in his arms, in bed and a few other interesting places, shimmering with enthusiasm and joy, turning to him with an eagerness that shook him to the core.

But he hadn't realized until now that she had only responded. She had never told him what she wanted. Not once, until today, had she made an overture, and even that had been said in a way that still required him to take the initiative. And three days ago she wouldn't have been surprised if he'd asked her to take her belongings back to her room. For the first time he wondered how hard it had been for her to take that first step.

Mac had always been good in math, and he decided that adding two and two gave them a big problem. One that they'd better deal with right now.

''Stacy?''

''Yes?''

He clamped his hands at her hips, in case she decided to leap away like a startled deer. "Was that so hard to say, that you want to make love?"

"Of course not!" The answer came quickly. Too quickly.

"Then why did you wait for more than twenty-four hours to say it? It rained yesterday afternoon."

"I don't know." She gave a slight shrug. "It just . . . didn't seem like the right time."

"Because we were so busy?" When she didn't answer, Mac gave a short laugh. "Yeah, we were real busy. Playing cards. I was so hot for you, I couldn't even remember what we were playing."

She looked up at him, her eyes wide. "You were?"

"Yeah. I wanted you so bad, I ached all the way down to my toes."

"Why on earth didn't you say something?"

"Because," he said bluntly, "I was watching you, and you wouldn't even look at me. I thought I had loved you too well, too often, and you were sore."

Stacy flushed. "I didn't want to be playing cards," she admitted, clearing her throat. "I wanted to be upstairs with you, and I was afraid that if I looked at you, you'd see it written all over my face."

"Why the hell shouldn't I see it?" he asked in an exasperated rumble.

"I don't know." She gave him an aggravated glance. "I told you it had been four years. Well, even before that, it was just a few times in college. They weren't real earth-shattering times, and I didn't learn a heck of a lot." She spoke quickly, gaining momentum with every word. "I don't know how to talk to a man about things like this. I don't know how to tell him I want him." She shot him a look of utter annoyance, telling him he'd be lucky if he ever heard those words from her.

Mac hugged her until she squeaked in protest, trying not to laugh. She was so damned serious about it all! "You crazy woman, I'm nuts about you." He set her back on his thighs and watched while her hair swung into place.

"First of all you're taking this too seriously," he assured her. "A man isn't very complicated. When he's around a woman he wants, he's usually thinking of one thing. So if you get the notion, you don't have to worry that you're going to shock him, because it's a sure thing that it's been on his mind a lot longer than it has on yours."

Stacy gave him a skeptical look.

He laughed. "If a man's real thick, a woman can say something subtle like, 'I want you. Now!' And more than likely he'll catch on." He touched her face with a gentle hand. "But you're right about one thing, if you looked at me, wanting me, you wouldn't have to say a word. It would be written all over your pretty face, and I'd love it. I'd also have you upstairs and out of your clothes before you knew what was happening."

Stacy blinked up at him thoughtfully.

His thumb stroked down her jawline and settled on the wild pulse in her throat. "But just once I think you need to say it as much as I need to hear it."

Thunder rumbled in the distance as Stacy looped her hands around his neck and tugged his head down. She brushed her lips over his, murmuring, "I want you, cowboy. Now."

Before he could move, she put a hand on his chest to stop him. Her green eyes laughing up at him, she said,

"If you'll give me a head start to the door, I bet I can beat you upstairs."

Mac grinned and opened his arms. Stacy jumped up and raced down the porch. When she reached the door, Mac was already on his feet, the swing bouncing wildly behind him. Laughing with excitement, she flew across the room and up the stairs, looking back when she reached the top. She let out a startled yelp when he scooped her up and tossed her over his shoulder.

He was right, she thought a minute later, lying in the middle of the bed where he had dropped her. He'd had her naked before she'd stopped laughing. And now, standing by the window as lightning ripped through the slate gray sky, Mac removed his clothes. Stacy rolled over onto her stomach, propping her chin on her folded arms, watching him.

He was beautiful, she thought again, watching him tug off his boots and socks. Beautiful. The shirt went next, revealing his sleek shoulders and arms, his chest outlined with the crisp markings of dark hair. The first time she had touched him, she had learned how hard he was. Now she knew that he was as tender as he was strong—and that he dealt equally well with both aspects.

He made quick work of his pants, unbuckled the belt, unsnapped the jeans, pushed them and his underwear down at the same time and stepped out of them. He left them where they were and walked toward her, lean hipped, long legged and undeniably male.

Stacy rolled onto her back, one knee bent, smiling at him, anticipation searing through her like a drumroll. One touch, she thought, that's all it takes, one touch of his lean fingers to start a fever in her body. Mac leaned over her, pressing his hands on the bed, one on either side of her shoulders, holding her a willing captive within the cage of his arms. Stacy, gazing up at his taut face, knew she was wrong. He didn't have to touch her. He had sensitized her to the point where it only took a look to make her body feel tight and empty.

She barely heard the thunder roll and crash over the house or the rain that sheeted down. Damp air carried the fragrance of wet trees and grass through the open windows, and Stacy shivered, wondering vaguely if it was Mac or the cool air that made her nipples hard and tight.

"Are you cold?" Mac's voice was a gentle rumble that made her shiver again.

Her eyes widened. "I don't know," she said honestly. "It could be you."

Mac straightened, grinning down at her. "You're good for my ego. Come on, let's get comfortable." He threw back the blanket, urged her beneath the sheet and eased down beside her. Tugging the pillows behind them, he settled back with a sigh, tucking Stacy in the curve of his arm. "You wanted a storm, and we've got a humdinger. Now we watch. And listen."

Stacy's brows rose. "That's all?"

"For a while."

Watching with Mac was a never-to-be-forgotten experience, Stacy decided a few minutes later. Listening wasn't so bad, either. Outside, the lightning put on a dazzling show, plunging across the sky in jagged streaks. The thunder grumbled and cracked, echoing across the big valley. Inside, the air was heavy and damp from the rain, but they were warm beneath the sheet.

Being next to Mac's big body was like cuddling with a furnace, Stacy thought, lazily tracing the outer edges of the hair on his chest. She was on her side, pressed against him from head to toes, with one hand free to explore as far as she could reach. And for all Mac's talk about listening and watching, he was doing his share of touching.

She stretched like a cat against him, sliding one of her legs between his, almost purring when his callused hand slowly moved down her back, his thumb tracing her spine. He cupped her bottom, shaping it with his hand, squeezing gently, tugging her closer against his hip.

Entranced by the textures of his body, Stacy snuggled closer, touching, stroking, tracing hard, unyielding muscles covered with smooth skin that still held a faint reminder of soap and the essence of man that was all Mac. His hair was springy and soft, inviting. She accepted the invitation, tracing down to the bottom of the triangle on his chest and following the dark, silky trail down his stomach.

"Do you like that?" she asked softly, spreading her hand over his belly and lacing her fingers through the heavier thatch of hair.

Mac groaned. "Sweetheart, if I liked it any more, I'd be melting all over you." He moved swiftly, gripping her hips with his hands and lifting her as if she weighed no more than a feather, settling her on his belly, grinning when she braced her hands on his chest and blinked down at him. He reached up and cupped her breasts, stroking her nipples with his thumbs, and asked, "You have a problem with this?"

Stacy closed her eyes, allowing her body to adjust to the new sensations: Mac's hard body between her thighs, his hands working magic on her breasts, the liquid fire sweeping through her veins, the tension in her loins building to unbearable proportions.

She shook her head. "No problem," she said weakly.

After three days with Mac, Stacy thought she knew what to expect. She was wrong; she had no idea. With his work-roughened hands, his eyes and his mouth he savored her, telling her she was perfect. Beautiful. Touching and stroking her legs, belly and breasts until she cried out, he built the storm within her until it was as great as the one without. Thunder crashed overhead and lightning dug deep inside her.

And Stacy, feeling both vulnerable and victorious, reached for him, claiming Mac with her body, gasping when he lifted her and then eased her back down on him. Exultantly she arched her back, sheathing him, tormenting him, sheltering him. And together they shimmered. Their bodies sang and soared, wild and free. And when the storm reached its zenith, demanding completion, she clung to him, shuddering, calling his name, hearing her own in return, feeling him deep within, his body bestowing a fulfillment and peace that she had never known.

To Mac she was perfect, silky and sexy. Entranced by her blazing sensuality, by the need and hunger in her that matched his own, he forgot everything but the stunning pleasure of the moment.

Afterward, exhausted, Stacy tucked her head under his chin and slept.

Mac's arms tightened convulsively around her, holding her so close she mumbled a sleepy protest. She was still on top of him, knees bent beside his hips. He was still deep within her.

He loosened his grip, cupping her shapely bottom with his hands, wishing he could sleep. Instead, he stared bleakly at the ceiling and decided it was time to pull his head out of the sand. He had spent his life facing hard facts, looking at options and figuring the odds—at least he had until last week when Stacy had burst into his life like a blazing comet. In that brief time, he hadn't had a rational thought, much less been able to plan for the future.

But now it was time to get his butt in gear.

He briefly closed his eyes in disgust, silently admitting that there was only one reason he hadn't been able to talk to Stacy—and it didn't have a damn thing to do with how much time they had spent in bed. For the first time in his life he had been afraid to tackle a problem head-on. He hadn't asked her one single thing about the past because he knew as sure as God made green apples it would inevitably lead to talking about the future.

And he didn't want to do that.

He didn't want to hear Stacy say she was leaving. He wanted even less to admit that the thought of it sent him into a panic. She was a woman with dreams, and it hurt like hell to know that he wasn't part of them. She was a woman on the run, and he was afraid he couldn't hold her.

There was a time bomb ticking away, and any day now Pete was going to call about the car and the damn thing was going to blow sky-high, taking him along with it.

He smoothed his hand up her back, hardening when she murmured and nestled closer.

All he needed was a plan.

It shouldn't be too hard to come up with one—if there was anything he was good at, it was plans. He was known throughout the county as the man who always had plans, ones that covered all the contingencies. Plans for the present and the future. Hell, up to a week ago, he'd even had a blueprint for a wife and kids.

Well, now he needed a new one—preferably one that would stop a running woman and give her a skyful of dreams. And he needed it quick.

Damned quick.

Ten

"All right, that's it!" Maxie spun around from the sink where she was peeling a mound of carrots, her hands on her hips, and turned exasperated blue eyes on Stacy. "Girl, you're jumpier than a flea on a griddle. That's the third potato you've slung across the floor. You're supposed to be peeling them for the stew, not bowling with them."

Stacy looked up and shrugged apologetically. "Sorry, Maxie, I guess my mind's wandering. I'll clean the floor."

"The floor isn't the problem," Maxie said bluntly. "You've been heaving sighs like they're free for the taking. If something's worrying you," she added in a softer voice, "I've got broad shoulders. I'm always willing to listen. And I don't tell that rapscallion cousin of mine everything I hear."

Stacy gave the older woman a swift hug. "Thanks, that means a lot."

"But you're not in the talking mood," Maxie said shrewdly.

"You're right. I'm not."

"Then go out and get some fresh air. Go talk to some of the boys and let them take you on another fool errand to find a power place." She picked up a carrot and went back to work, sending a shower of orange shavings into the sink. "I never thought to ask, did you find anything at Doc's place? The one that Slim told you about?"

Stacy shook her head. "I'm batting zero, so far. Of course, I've heard a lot of interesting stories and seen some nice places, so it hasn't been a total loss."

Maxie snorted. "I'm beginning to think they're making these things up just so they can get you alone in one of the trucks."

"I'm not so sure. It can be a hot spot for them and not affect me. After all, everyone can't have the same power place, or we'd all be piled up in one section of the globe. Besides, if that's what they're doing, I don't know why they bother, because they've all treated me like a queen. They're some of the nicest men I've ever met."

"And if they value their hides, that's just the way they'll stay. Mac won't put up with any trouble from them, especially not where you're concerned." She stopped, but when Stacy apparently had nothing to say, she went on with brusque kindness. "You need some fresh air, so go on, go find something to do. Scat!"

Stacy started to scat but was stopped halfway out the door when Maxie called her name. She stuck her head back in the kitchen. "You rang, madam?"

Maxie seemed to be addressing the carrot in her hand rather than Stacy when she muttered, "I just wondered if... Has Pete called about your car?"

The silence in the room was getting oppressive when Stacy finally answered, very gently. "No. Pete hasn't called yet."

And that, of course, was the problem, Stacy reflected seconds later as she walked automatically over the hill behind the house, heading for the grotto. He hadn't, but just as inevitably as death and the IRS on April fifteenth, he would.

And they were all waiting. They were also walking on eggshells. At least, she and Mac were, as well as Maxie, in her own peculiar way.

It had been a week since she'd made the best decision of her life, since she'd gathered every bit of courage she possessed and moved into Mac's room. A week of revelation and enchantment. Of teasing, laughter, companionship, great sex and love.

All it had lacked was honesty.

And since honesty was a basic building block for any relationship, they obviously didn't have one. What they did have, she concluded miserably, was a situation with two people who liked each other, who even loved each other, who were scared to death to discuss any matter that even verged on the personal.

Mac wouldn't ask questions, and she was afraid to reveal information. It left him with a lot of silence, her with even more half lies. It was definitely not a situation conducive to developing a meaningful relationship. Or a marriage.

Thrusting her hands into the pockets of her shorts, Stacy fingered the small, polished stones she had taken from the basket that morning. It had quickly become a habit to drop a few in her pockets each day before she left the room. Rubbing the glossy pebbles between her fingers had also become a habit, one that gave her new insights into the custom of some Europeans to carry worry beads. For whatever reason, the stones evoked an image of the grotto, bringing the presence of the cool, running water to mind, the sun-warmed boulders, the whispers and darting shadows of the leafy trees. All in all, it was a soothing pastime, one that calmed her nerves.

It was also an appropriate one these days, she decided, ducking under a low-hanging branch, because her stress level was running off the charts.

She hopped over the small stream onto the picnic-size boulder and got down on her hands and knees to pull the quilt out of a hole she had discovered several days earlier. The stash was a long stretch under a low, overhanging lip, but it kept the blanket dry and saved her hauling it back and forth, so she didn't mind the inconvenience.

With her cheek resting on the rock and her bottom in the air, she reached for the quilt. Just as her fingers touched the fabric, a large, warm hand slid over her bottom. The touch was as startling as it was intimate.

Her yelp startled the birds into a frenzied flight. She banged her head on the lip of the boulder and saw stars. She also swore, her temper getting the best of her when Mac laughed. Rolling away from the overhang, she was stopped by his boots.

"Dammit, Mac," she yelled, sitting up and swishing her hair out of her eyes, "I've had it with you sneaking up on me! You scared a year's growth out of me, and I don't have that much to spare. I've asked you over and over not to do that. And how you manage in those great, clomping boots is beyond me. Any normal man would—''

''I'm sorry.''

Her eyes narrowed to green slits at the tremor in his voice. ''The hell you are! If you were, you'd quit doing it.''

''Let me help you up.''

She batted away the hand he held out to her, glaring at him militantly as adrenaline flooded her body. ''Don't do me any favors, okay? I don't need your help, what's more, I don't *want* your help. I'm fine, just fine, right here.'' She folded her arms across her chest and took a deep breath for the next salvo. ''Why don't you go on with whatever you were going to do? I'll just sit here and wait for the bump on my head to go down.''

Stacy knew she was overreacting. She knew she was being irrational and unfair. That her temper was partly due to stress, a lot to guilt. None of that mattered. It felt so good to sit and blow off steam, she planned to keep right on doing it.

But she hadn't counted on Mac losing *his* temper.

His face hardened, and she was looking at a colder version of the man she'd lived with for the past week, one with narrowed eyes and thinned lips. He reached down, clamped his hands under her armpits and hauled her to her feet as if she weighed no more than a hummingbird. He set her down with a thump and said one word through his clenched teeth. ''Stay!''

''I'm not a dog,'' she said to the top of his head as he hunkered down and hauled out the quilt. He tossed her a cold look that told her she'd better not budge, then stalked over and spread the quilt on a bed of needles at the base of a tall pine.

She was going to march away out of sheer orneriness, but before she could decide where to go, he was back. He tossed her over his shoulder like a sack of feed and carried her across the water, clamping his hand on the back of her thighs. When he reached the quilt, he none too gently set her on her feet, sat down with his back against the tree and tumbled her down into his lap.

Stacy sat there, rigid with temper until he wrapped an arm beneath her breasts and pulled her back against him. "What do you think you're *doing?*" She wiggled and squirmed, but it didn't do her a bit of good.

He tightened his arm. "You told me to keep on doing what I was going to do. Well, this is what I came for. To hold you. But I didn't know that when I got my hands on you, I'd want to throttle you. Now hush up and let me get my temper in hand."

Stacy used the next few minutes to calm down herself. She supposed her meditation techniques would work, but she was too rattled to try. Instead, she reached into her pocket and withdrew several of the polished stones, rolling them between her fingers.

Long before she was ready, Mac sighed and said, "Lord, sweetheart, I didn't know you had such a temper."

Stacy rubbed one of the stones between her thumb and finger as a line from a childhood game running through her mind—*ready or not, here I come*. Well, she wasn't ready, but the time for a little honesty had definitely come. "There's a lot you don't know about me," she said quietly.

"And whose fault is that?"

"Mine," she said. "All mine."

He touched her hand, the one with the stones. "I'm here. I don't want to strangle you anymore. I'll be here for as long as it takes. I'm listening."

Wondering where to begin, Stacy warned, "It's a dull story."

"Doesn't matter, as long as it's *your* story. The whole thing, not just the bits and pieces you pull out for public consumption."

"There aren't any villians, no high drama. Just ordinary people."

Mac settled back more comfortably against the tree, hugging her closer, holding her in the cradle of his bent knees. "Quit stalling."

"I was an only child," she said abruptly. "Well loved and probably a little spoiled. Daddy owned the label factory, the biggest business in town. Actually, the family owned it. My aunts and uncles invested their savings in it. What they had, combined with the money my parents had, bought the place. They knew Daddy was a sharp cookie, and if anyone could provide for their old age, he could."

She looked out over the tumbling water, her thoughts drifting back over the years. "The factory was my second home. I knew every one of its nooks and crannies. When I was old enough to work, I started at the bottom and, over the years, worked at almost every position. Doing vacation relief and helping out when someone was sick, things like that."

"What about Prudence?" Mac asked.

"A nice town, with nice people. It never changed."

"But you did?"

"Ah. Yeah." She absently kneaded his thigh with her fingers. "I had a hunger to see the rest of the country, to know what other people were like. My parents understood. They promised that when I went to college, I could go anywhere I wanted. I started collecting college catalogs when I was fourteen."

"So where did you go?" Mac nudged, more to break her pensive silence than because he was impatient.

"Right after my high school graduation, my mother died. It was sudden and left Daddy and me... floundering. I didn't want to leave him alone, so I drove back and forth to a college thirty miles away."

"So you did go?" He smiled, thinking about the pottery and karate.

"Oh, yeah. The uncles and aunts clustered around and made sure I did. I even got myself a big-time diploma."

"Liberal arts?" he asked tactfully.

"M.B.A." Stacy felt him jerk, and she grinned for the first time since she'd begun. "I found I had a knack for it," she said simply. "During those years, we healed and once again, my big adventure was going to begin after I graduated. I was going to have a glamorous job in a big city. That was four years ago."

Mac felt her tense and knew what she was going to say. He closed his eyes and waited.

"Daddy died," she said simply. "And aside from the pain, the timing was rotten. He had taken a risk, expanding the factory in a bad economy. Things were bad. If the company folded, the town would fold. And my aunts and uncles would be broke. So I stepped in. It...wasn't easy."

Mac winced, remembering he had planned to give her a lecture on responsibility and commitment.

"It was hard for my dad's business associates to accept me as his replacement. They had watched me grow up and remembered the harum-scarum kid. So I dressed for success, business suits, briefcase and my hair in a bun. I was Ms. Sullivan, dull and drab enough to satisfy the most ultra of conservatives.''

"A bun?'' He ran his hand over her silky hair. "What a waste.''

"Maybe, but it helped. Anyway, the bottom line is, I am very good at what I do. I worked my buns off, beefed up the plant, made it a very attractive prospect, found a buyer who would not only pay what I wanted, but would keep the people in town employed. My aunts and uncles are set for the rest of their lives, and I got my freedom.''

Freedom. Mac felt a chill crawling up his spine. There was that damn word again. To distract himself, he asked the question that had been driving him crazy since the first night they made love. "Are all the men in Prudence blind? Or gelded? Or dead? Four years and not one of them got close to you?''

She looked up at him over her shoulder. "You'd feel better if one of them had?''

"Hell, no!'' He scowled down at her. "I just don't understand how they kept their hands off you.''

Stacy gave him a wry smile. "Ah, McClain, where were you when I needed you? Those were very long years. But I have to admit, it was my fault. I dressed in a way that encouraged it.''

"That's no excuse,'' he said, sounding disgusted. "I would have seen the fire in you whatever you wore.''

She silently agreed with him; he probably would have. "It was more than clothes, it was an...attitude, for want of a better word. I was the only female executive in a very small, conservative town. I had to meet the men on their terms. I had to be credible. I was trying to keep a company alive and a town employed, and I was handicapped. I was a woman. The men I dealt with wouldn't have taken me seriously if I had involved myself in the usual dating and mating games."

"That a lot of—"

"You're right," 'she said hastily, "but that's the way it was. And since I had a goal—to sell at a good profit—I knew it wouldn't be forever. So I wore my pin-striped suits, and I made damn sure that no one ever saw me looking anything less than the efficient, sexless president of SullCo. It was a pretty good act and, eventually, everyone bought into it."

"Including Stacy Sullivan?"

Stacy deliberately loosened the grip of her fingers on his leg and blinked back the tears that burned her eyes. He had cut right to the core, and she was shaken by both his perception and the incredible tenderness in his voice.

"Yeah," she said huskily, "including me."

Mac touched her throat; then his large hand framed her head, his fingers lacing through her silky hair. "What happened after you sold the company?" he asked lazily, deliberately diverting her. "Did you really have a yard sale?"

"The biggest in the county," she said promptly, smiling reminiscently. "And then I tried to make up for the long drought. I bought a new image. New clothes, new makeup, books I hadn't had time to read and a snazzy new haircut." Her fingers tangled with his when she reached up to touch her hair.

Mac captured her hand and bent his head to kiss her fingertips, one by one. When he finished the task to his satisfaction, he looked down at her flushed cheeks. "You didn't buy a new image," he said definitely. "You just encouraged the real Stacy to come out and play."

Shaken once again by his perception, Stacy still managed to keep her tone light. "A cowboy psychologist, just what you'd expect to find in the wilds of Arizona."

"A tired cowboy psychologist," he agreed, sitting up abruptly and lifting Stacy over his leg to the quilt beside him. He slid down until he was flat on his back, one hand folded beneath his head, the other extended to Stacy. "We got very little rest last night, love. Come take a nap with me."

Stacy looked down at him, considering the offer. Mac did look tired, she decided. And he was right, they had gotten very little sleep, not just last night but for the whole week.

Strictly to help him sleep, she slid down and curled up against him, settling her head on his shoulder and draping her arm across his chest. Smiling at the weight of his arm around her, she was astounded when a huge yawn overtook her. Confession, she decided groggily. It was not only good for the soul, it took a big weight off the body. In less than a minute she was sound asleep.

Mac lay for a long time just holding her, staring up at the swaying treetops, wondering how he was going to hold a bird that was hell-bent on flying free.

"Do you have any jeans?" Mac finished his coffee and put his mug on the table just in time for Maxie to sweep it away with the other remnants of supper.

Stacy nodded. "Sure. Why? Don't you like my shorts?" She looked down, silently admitting that they might be just a tad bright, but the watermelon pink was probably her favorite.

"Love them," Mac said promptly. "Great color. But I want to show you something, and I . . . don't want you to get cold. Oh, and wear some tennis shoes, okay?"

"Mac." She eyed his bland face suspiciously. "I want you to remember that while I come from a small town, I'm basically a city girl. I don't find things like rattlers' nests entertaining."

He looked astounded. "Why the hell would I want to take you to a nest of rattlers, assuming I even knew where to find one?"

"I don't know." She lifted her shoulders in a slight shrug. "But since your cowboys took me to visit the places where they've had weird and wonderful experiences, I have a feeling that Westerners have a unique definition of entertainment."

She was serious. Mac studied her earnest green eyes and saw that she was definitely serious. "Now, honey," he soothed, "you know I'd never do anything to hurt you. Trust me on this, okay."

She gave him a skeptical look. "Okay, but just for the record, the last man who gave me that *trust me* line, was trying to sell the modern equivalent of snake oil. Be back in a minute."

Watching the unconsciously seductive sway of her hips as she walked out the door, Mac's grin faded to something far more basic. Her smile and brilliant green eyes held the same promise as her body, he reflected—innocence, honesty and a slam of sensuality that knocked a man to his knees.

And she was his.

She had given herself to him with the fierce passion of an Amazon, with breathtaking honesty and an innocent wonder that burned a man to cinders even as he dreamed dreams and looked for dragons to slay. It also made a man's jeans fit tight when he thought about her doing it again, Mac thought wryly, getting up and prowling restlessly around the room.

He was mulling over the twist of fate that joined a trucker, an elf and a pragmatic cowboy when she danced back into the room, clad in eye-popping purple.

"Great color," he said for the second time that evening, wondering if there was a single ordinary piece of clothing in her wardrobe. If there was, he hadn't seen it.

"Where are we going?" she demanded as he led her out the back door.

"It's a surprise." He wondered how long it would take her to figure out that they were headed for the barn and remember that there were horses in the barn, as well as saddles and bridles.

Not long at all.

When Slim stepped out of the barn leading the gray gelding that was Mac's favorite mount, Stacy dug her heels into the dirt.

"Mac, we've been through this before," she said through gritted teeth. "You are not going to stick me on one of those giants. I don't like heights, and I don't know how to steer them."

Slim came to a stop when he reached them. "Now, Tumbleweed, you just have to give it a chance."

"Don't 'Tumbleweed' me, you traitor! How could you bring that thing out for me when you know I—"

"He didn't." Mac's deep voice stopped her, and she watched him step into the stirrup and swing up in one lithe movement. "He brought him for me." He waited for her to give an explosive sigh of relief before he grinned and said, "You're the passenger."

Stacy blinked up at him, curiosity and intrigue gleaming in her wide eyes. Mac groaned. It was the same expression he'd seen the first night they had made love, when she'd looked at him like a kid eyeing candy in a store, knowing she could have whatever she wanted.

"Passenger? You mean I don't have to do it alone?"

"Nope. I wouldn't do that to you, much less to one of my horses."

"Do I do it in front or in back?"

Mac avoided Slim's gaze and his grin. It was going to be sweet torture either way. If she sat behind him, her breasts would be poking into his back. In front, her bottom would be pressing right against him. He was a glutton for punishment, he decided. And what was worse, he couldn't wait to get started.

"The front," he told her. "That way you can see where we're going." He eased to the back of the saddle, leaving her a little room, knowing she was going to be sliding into him every step of the way. "Give her a boost up, Slim." He held the horse steady while she came up in an awkward scramble and settled in front of him.

"We're very high," Stacy observed anxiously, clutching the arm he had wrapped around her waist when the horse began to move. "I hope he isn't accident-prone."

"Don't worry about the horse," he told her. "I'll take care of him. Feel the way I'm moving and try to move with me."

A few minutes later, when nothing dire had happened, Stacy relaxed enough to ease back against Mac's hard body. "Well," she allowed cautiously, "it's not as bad as I thought it would be."

"Don't worry, Silver," Mac said to the horse. "That's high praise from a city slicker. She really likes you."

Diverted, Stacy turned laughing eyes up at Mac. "Silver? You didn't really."

He shrugged, the corners of his mouth turning up in a grin. "Why not? It's an okay name. Besides, I grew up listening to the Lone Ranger."

"That kind of reasoning just proves what my aunt always says."

"I know I'm going to hate myself for asking, but what does your aunt always say?"

"That boys just grow up to be bigger boys."

"Well, she just might be right," he drawled. "Some of us do get to be pretty big. You've pointed that out to me more than once."

"Mac!" Stacy primmed her mouth, pretending to be shocked. "That's terrible."

"Silver, old fella, are you listening to this? It just shows how quick a woman changes her mind. Only last night she told me I was wonderful. And beautiful. And even—" He stopped with a grin when Stacy jabbed him in the ribs with her elbow.

Mac hugged her tighter, rubbing his cheek in her gorgeous, silky hair and dropping a kiss on her nape. His eyes narrowed in satisfaction when she shivered. "I just may make a career out of teasing you," he decided. "Your eyes sparkle, your cheeks get pink and you relax enough to ride a horse exactly the way it should be ridden."

Stacy looked up at him, studying his bland expression. "You're a devious man, McClain," she finally said. "I suppose your horse's name isn't really Silver."

Amusement glimmered in his dark eyes. "Well, no. Actually, it's Gray."

"Talk about going from the sublime to the prosaic," she muttered. "You could have at least called him Smoky or Slate."

They rode on, the silence broken only by the sound of Gray's hooves on the stony ground and the distant tapping of a woodpecker. High overhead came the shrill cry of a hawk making one last foray before dusk.

"Why are we out here, Mac?" It was a lazy question, not a complaint.

"Two reasons. First, I wanted to get you on a horse."

"Why?"

He shrugged. "Because I knew you'd like it. Besides," he added blandly, "I knew you had great potential as a rider."

Stacy studied his face with narrowed eyes that rounded quite suddenly when she recalled several shameless incidents that might have encouraged the belief. Knowing that her cheeks were undoubtedly pinker than her blouse, she gave Mac a punishing pinch on his hard thigh.

"Ouch," he said obligingly, grinning down at her.

"What's the second reason?" she asked with a resigned sigh. The man was clearly impossible!

"I wanted you to see the land the way it should be seen. Away from trucks and roads."

The simple words were enough for the time being. They rode contentedly, moving to higher ground as they had done since they'd left the house. They eventually came to a point that overlooked the valley and foothills, with towering, slate blue peaks in the distance.

Mac drew the horse to a halt a safe distance from the edge and gazed silently at the panoramic view, wondering what Stacy was thinking. Look at it! he wanted to shout. Touch it, smell it, feel it, let it be a part of your blood and bones the way it is mine. Say one word, give me one look, and it's yours, babe, along with me and everything else I own.

That was what he wanted to say, but this valiant woman in his arms had sacrificed too many dreams for other people, too many times. He wanted her with every drop of blood in his body, and he didn't know how he would survive if she left, but he wasn't going to use emotional blackmail to keep her there. Because even worse than the dread of loss was the fear that if she stayed, she would always look at the horizon with long-ing eyes, wondering what was beyond the mountains.

"It's so vast," Stacy murmured. "So beautiful."

"Most of it is McClain land," he said steadily. "It's good land—hard but good. And it's big enough not to crowd people, to let them grow the way they want to grow, to be exactly what they want to be. It's a good place to live."

During the night, Stacy turned over and opened her eyes. Mac was on his back, his hands folded beneath his head. He slept naked, and the bright moonlight made a stark contrast between his dark skin and the white sheets.

Laying her hand on his arm, she said softly, "Are you awake?"

"Yeah." He reached out and tugged her against him, seeing as well as feeling the difference between her soft, honey-tanned body and his hard one. She sighed and nuzzled his throat with her lips.

Stacy took a deep breath, as if preparing to dive off a cliff into turbulent water far below. "I just want you to know," she told him in a shaky voice, "I never ex-pected to find a man like you. Those years in Prudence I did a lot of dreaming and fantasizing, but I could never even imagine someone like you."

She slid down, resting her cheek on his chest, and his heart almost stopped when he felt her hot tears. "I love you, Evan McClain. I love you with all my heart and soul."

Mac turned over, taking her with him and pinning her against the mattress. He smoothed her hair back from her face and when he saw her tear-drenched eyes, he felt his heart turn over.

"Eight days ago I stepped out of my truck and saw sunshine and laughter sitting on the hood of a car," he told her, brushing her lips with his. The tenderness in his voice made her tears flow harder. "I lost my heart, babe, and I'll never get it back. I'm here, so put your arms around me and hold on to the man who loves you from here to heaven and back, from now until forever."

Eleven

———

"Maxie?"

Stacy walked into the quiet kitchen, not really expecting to see the older woman. She had noticed the silence that pervaded the entire house as soon as she left their room. She stopped, distracted, blinking thoughtfully at her choice of words. *Their* room, not Mac's. Her brows rose in speculation as she considered the ramifications of her automatic claim. Plural and possessive. Maybe they did have a relationship, she thought with a burst of optimism.

Having established that, she circled back to the original question, the whereabouts of Maxie. Maxie carried with her an innate sense of bustle, Stacy thought with a grin, so if she was close at hand, you heard her. She might be humming off-key, muttering over a recipe or yelling orders out of the kitchen window, but one way or another, you heard her.

Having reached the tidy conclusion that Maxie was not in the house, Stacy spotted the note on the kitchen table that verified it. Maxie was at a neighbor's house where a group had convened for some cutthroat bridge. She would see Stacy later. All the men were gone, chasing horses from one valley to another, and wouldn't be back until around suppertime.

Stacy poured herself a cup of coffee, remembering Mac's good-morning kiss at dawn. It had been a lingering kiss, one that was escalating nicely when they heard Curly calling to the men in the bunkhouse. Mac had groaned, sworn with exasperation and tossed the covers back. While he dressed he mentioned that he would be gone for the day and suggested she get some rest. One last kiss, a slow, smooth run of his hand over her bare bottom, and he was gone.

Stacy rummaged through the huge, old-fashioned bread box Maxie kept in the pantry and pulled out a poppy-seed muffin left over from yesterday's breakfast. She took it back in the kitchen, collected her coffee and sat down at the table, breaking off a piece and popping it into her mouth. Ambrosia, she decided. Sheer heaven.

Of course, Maxie would have a fit if she saw what she was eating, Stacy reflected, pouring some cream into her coffee. She would insist that it wasn't enough, that there was no protein. It had developed into an ongoing dialogue between them. Stacy didn't like big meals, and for some reason, Maxie's mission in life was apparently to stuff her like a Christmas goose.

Stacy was chewing the last bite of muffin, considering her good fortune when the telephone rang. She picked it up and said a bit thickly, "McClain's."

"Mornin'," a cheerful masculine voice said. "Can I talk to Stacy Sullivan?"

Stacy swallowed. "This is she."

"This is Pete. Good news. I got the circuit board yesterday, and your car's ready to go. I'll have it out there in about an hour. Will you be there?"

"Yes."

"What? Sorry, an eighteen wheeler just went by. I didn't hear you."

"I said, yes. Fine. I'll be here. Thank you." Stacy dropped the phone in the cradle and gazed around the room, her heart beating as rapidly as if she had been running for her life.

It was too soon, she thought dazedly. One day too soon. He'd said ten days, and they'd only had nine, she thought with a sudden rush of panic. She wanted that extra day. She had counted on it, dammit!

She needed it.

And what would she gain if she had it? she wondered bleakly. A few more visits to the grotto? More time in which to involve herself in the rhythm and fabric of Mac's life? The certainty that she should leave? The knowledge that she would never go?

She automatically rinsed her cup and put it into the dishwasher before walking upstairs. When she opened the bedroom door, she felt Mac's presence with an actual, physical pain.

Stacy stepped in, looking around Mac's room at her own possessions scattered rather carelessly around—a book on the bedside table, a magazine in the chair, her sandals by the desk. She recalled her promise when she had moved in, to keep her things out of sight. Mac had surveyed his room, a small smile on his face and possession in his eyes, saying he liked it just as it was.

Once again Stacy stopped, considering her unspoken words. *Mac's* room. *His* room.

The decision, it seemed, had already been made, but it was hard to begin. Finally, Stacy stepped into the closet and ruthlessly reached for her clothes. She was packed in less than an hour.

The hardest part was writing the note.

She was loading the last few things in the car when Maxie pulled up. Instead of driving to the rear as she normally would, she stopped beside the red Buick and jumped out.

"So you're really going to do it," she said brusquely. "You're leaving."

Stacy nodded, pushing a tote bag into place.

"Where to?"

"I don't know." Stacy finally turned to face her friend and realized that she *didn't* know. The only thing she did know was that she had to leave.

Now.

"Will you be back?" The anxious look on Maxie's face shattered Stacy's fragile thread of control.

"I don't know," she repeated, this time in a whisper. Her shrug came a split second before the tears that spilled down her cheeks.

"Oh, baby." Maxie enveloped her in a hug, the kind of hug that women have always given each other when they sought to console or share grief. "Why are young people so hard on themselves?"

"You'll take care of him?" Stacy wiped her eyes with a soggy tissue.

"I always have. Dammit!" Maxie kicked a rock with the toe of one gray boot. "I knew it. You're gonna break his heart."

"I'm leaving mine in its place." Stacy turned the key in the ignition and tried to smile at her agitated friend. It was a miserable attempt.

"Fat lot of good that is," Maxie muttered, wiping her cheek with the back of her hand as the red car rocketed down the dirt road. "That one's broken, too."

"Hey, boss," Curly shouted over the tumult of the whinnying horses, "are they going, too?" He pointed to a cluster of mares several hundred feet behind Mac.

Mac looked at him. "Why wouldn't they?"

Curly laughed. "Damned if I know," he admitted cheerfully. "But since you're just sitting there smiling at them instead of chasing them this way, I thought maybe you'd changed your mind."

"I wasn't smiling at them," Mac explained carefully. "I was communicating with them on a deeper level."

"Oh." Curly's smile grew broader. "Well, tell them to hustle their butts, will you? We're just about through here." He rode off, whistling tunelessly. When he reached Slim, he said, "You know, we just might have a wife and kids on the ranch yet!"

Mac prodded his horse over to the lollygagging mares and hustled them along, moving automatically, his thoughts with Stacy. She looked so tempting in the morning, with her silky hair spread on the pillow and her body warm and rosy. And when she smiled and opened green eyes filled with teasing invitation, it made a man feel like hell on wheels in bed.

And it made getting out of bed about as attractive as a case of hives.

Last night she had been so...emotional. He shrugged, wondering if a man ever understood a woman. One minute she was flowing all over him, tempting and teasing until he though he'd explode. The next, she was shedding tears on his chest and almost stopping his heart.

But she loved him. Him. She'd said it loud and clear, so there were no doubts. She wouldn't leave now. He didn't have to worry about that damned red car coming back. She loved him and even if she had wings, she wouldn't fly away.

They would travel. He could hire a couple more hands to take up the slack and turn more over to Curly. He'd show her all the things she thought she'd missed. Hell, he'd even read that book and go hunting power places with her if that's what she wanted. And as far as finding that inner woman, somehow he'd have to convince her that she'd already tapped into the source; that on a scale of one to ten, she leveled out at about fifteen plus.

She loved him. He lived on the promise for the rest of the day, and by the time they straggled back to the ranch he had come up with a few creative suggestions in case she was inclined to prove it.

He took care of his horse and headed for the house, his plans for the evening basic: a shower, Stacy, food and Stacy. Not even noticing that Maxie wasn't banging pans in the kitchen, he took the stairs two at a time, calling ahead.

"Stacy?"

Mac stood in the open door, a chill working up his spine. The room was still and sterile. His furniture, *his* things were there, but nothing that belonged to Stacy. No sandals carelessly stepped out of, no how-to books, no magazines, no basket overflowing with stones. She was too neat to leave her clothes lying around, but he knew with certainty that they were gone, too. He stepped inside, stopping long enough to open and slam the dresser drawers before stalking to the closet. One look told him everything he needed to know.

She was gone.

Damn her to hell and back, she was *gone!*

Fury, pure and fierce, flooded him. She couldn't wait to get out of there. She hated the place so much, she couldn't wait. No goodbyes, no "thanks, it's been fun," not a single, damn thing. She just packed her clothes and left.

He strode over to the hall door and slammed it, shutting out the rest of the house, closing himself in with the only thing left, the faint, elusive, utterly feminine scent of Stacy Sullivan.

It was when he turned to look out the window that he saw the note on his desk. A white piece of paper, folded over with his name written in red ink, surrounded by polished stones placed in the shape of a heart.

Feeling as if he had received a blow to the heart, Mac picked up the note, careful not to jostle any of the stones. When he opened it, her writing leapt out at him in a surge of pain—hers, his, impossible to tell the difference.

Mac, my only love,
I thought I could make it work. But it won't, it truly won't. We had the right man, the right woman but the wrong time.
    Oh, my love, you deserve so much more than a woman with a gypsy soul. Find the one you need, the right one.

                                            Stacy

Mac read the note a second time, then a third, and when he finished he only knew that she was gone. Hurting as much as he was, but gone. She had cried while writing it, he saw, touching the last line where the red ink was blurred. Turning to look out the window, he wondered if those tears had been as hot as the ones that had seared his chest last night.

He didn't know his hand was clenched, he didn't know he was swinging, until the side of his fist shattered the glass before him.

"Dammit!"

Stacy cried all the way to Sedona. She stood on the massive red rocks, remembered what the ranch hands had said about UFOs and crystals and cried some more. She cried when she looked down from the South Rim of the Grand Canyon at the shining ribbon that was the Colorado River. She took a boat ride on Lake Powell and watched apathetically as the red rock sculptures glided by.

There's nothing more pathetic than a woman with tears dripping off her chin, she decided somewhere around Salt Lake City. She had gone through four boxes of tissues and had nothing to show for her effort except a headache and a raw nose. Aunt Tabby, had she been in the car, would have clucked and said it was past time to pull up her socks and get on with it. Whatever *it* was.

So Stacy reached for the CB and flipped it on. "Hi, are there any truckers out there who remember Tumbleweed? I'm on the road again."

"Hey, Tumbleweed!" A deep, syrupy drawl cut through the static. "My handle's Country Boy. Long John told me to keep my ears peeled for you. Understand you had a visit with Gibraltar. How'd it go?"

"Just...fine. He's a—" she took a deep breath "—nice man. Everyone at the ranch was. Nice, I mean. But my car's fixed, and I'm off and running."

"Where you heading?"

"Darned if I know. I just want to see what there is to see. Got any suggestions?"

"Well, I'm on I 15 heading north to Butte, Montana, and there's sure some pretty country between here and there."

"Sounds good to me. I think I'll tag along."

"Great. Touch base every now and then, and I'll warn you away from the flea pits and the barf bags."

"It's a deal, Country Boy. Thanks."

And so, for the next couple of days, she meandered north, resisting the temptation to call the ranch each time she passed a telephone box. She determindly played tourist in Salt Lake City, Pocatello and Butte, while she wondered if Mac was all right. There, a smooth-talking cross-country driver called Fritz sang the glories of I 90 west. "Hey, Tumbleweed, you have to see Seattle, then take a ferry over to the San Juan Islands."

She obediently turned west, moving farther away from Mac with every mile.

Days passed into weeks as truckers played tour guides, recommending the local sights and motels. She saw the rain forest and Mount St. Helens in Washington and worried about Mac. She avoided the bears at Crater Lake, watched the sun set from the rugged shores in Oregon and wondered about her sanity.

Stacy zigzagged across California, slipping across the border to play the slot machines at Lake Tahoe and cried when she hit a jackpot. She sampled wine in the rolling hills of the wine country, stayed in bed-and-breakfasts on Highway 49 in the gold rush towns, trying to recall what she had said in the frantic note she'd left for Mac— wondering if she had made any sense at all.

She visited Yosemite and, while she watched climbers struggle up the rock face of Half Dome, admitted that she was still miserable. That frightened her as much as it annoyed her.

She was supposed to be having fun, dammit! She was free. This was her dream. She was independent, unfolding and heading down 101 to the original fast-lane track. She was having the vacation of a lifetime.

She was still miserable.

Stacy arrived in Los Angeles at three in the afternoon and learned about gridlock. She was terrified by the freeway system and awed by the drivers. When traffic moved, they swooped and scuttled and *always* stayed cool. But then, they knew where they were going, she reasoned, shuddering when a semi roared by her with just inches to spare. She picked up a couple of shiny stones from the basket beside her and rubbed them for good luck.

When she grabbed for the CB and called for help, a woman trucker with a foghorn voice, named Big Mama, held her hand. "Hell, honey," she bellowed cheerfully, "there's nothing you can do about this mess except ride it out. Just stick a tape in the deck and take your mind off the traffic. Books are good, a mystery's the best. Where'd you say you're from, honey, Missouri?"

Stacy winced as a car edged in front of her in a space she would have sworn couldn't handle a scooter.

"Kansas."

"Well, you know best, of course, but I don't think this is the place for you. There's some mighty weird people around here. I made a pit stop yesterday and saw a gal with purple hair standing straight up and a bone through her nose. Don't imagine you see much of that in Montana."

"Kansas."

"Yeah. Tell you what, honey, you get on I 5 and follow it south about a hundred miles to La Jolla. It's a real pretty little place with flowerpots on the streets and all. Now it may be a little tricky looking for the sign, because people back in Nebraska don't understand how we spell out here. It has a *j* and two *l*'s."

Stacy blinked and moved ahead about three feet. "What does?"

"The name of the *town*."

"All right," Stacy said numbly, wondering where a place that sounded like La Hoya hid two *l*'s and a *j*. "I'll watch for it."

"When you get there, go to this cute little motel just outside of town. Just tell 'em Big Mama sent you, and they'll give you a cut rate. Good luck, honey."

Fortunately traffic had slowed to a stop, and Stacy was able to jot down the address and detailed instructions. "Thanks, I'll do it. I'm looking for a place to settle for a few days."

Big Mama was right, she thought several hours later as she opened the door of her room. The motel was picturesque, a pink, single-story structure abounding with white trellises covered in flowering vines. Vibrant impatiens and begonias tumbled out of huge pots that lined the walkway and entries. Stacy had been directed toward the end of the building where she shared a flower-bedecked porch with the last room.

The town was equally, if a bit self-consciously, lovely. Flowers were everywhere. They cascaded from hanging pots on the lampposts and swayed in planters attached to the elegant boutiques that lined the streets. For two days she investigated stores and strolled through the coastline parks.

The third day she wallowed in misery.

Swimming laps in the motel pool that evening, she admitted that she was lonely. Not just lonely, she decided, it was more than that. She was solitary, isolated. She didn't know a soul in the entire state of California. Or Oregon or Washington or Idaho or Utah. If anything happened to her—if for instance, she drowned in this damned pool—she'd probably be listed as a Jane Doe and buried in a...wherever they buried unknowns.

Thoroughly depressed, Stacy hauled herself out of the pool and picked up her towel. Rubbing her hair as she walked back to her room, she told herself that what she needed was a plan, an agenda for the next few days. An hour later she had showered, blown her hair dry, ordered a pizza, looked at maps and still didn't have a clue.

It wasn't that there weren't places to go, she acknowledged, she just didn't want to drive anymore. Five weeks was long enough; she was bone-tired.

Stacy glanced at the phone and had to clasp her hands in her lap. She ached to make one call. To one number. One place. One man. Hear one voice. Each night the temptation was greater, the pain worse.

She glanced back at the map and knew that there was one place she could go. She'd pack the car in a minute and take off. As far as that went, she'd walk barefoot on broken glass if she thought it would do any good.

But she had severed that link as swiftly and easily as a knife slides through soft butter, and there was no going back. She was sitting on the edge of the bed, thinking of dreams and a whole world of hurt, when someone thumped on the door.

Startled, she called out, "Who is it?"

"Pizza delivery."

Stacy looked down at her aqua shorts and shirt and headed for the door. Then, remembering that she wasn't in Prudence anymore, she turned on the porch light and squinted through the peephole. A teenager stood there with a flat, square box. She threw open the door—and sucked in her breath so quickly she almost choked.

Hanging in the center of the doorway from a length of fishing line, just at eye-level, was a red, glossy stone. Heart thudding, and hardly able to breathe, she touched it with fingers that trembled.

"Lady?"

Stacy looked at him and knew by his patient expression it wasn't the first time he had spoken.

"This is going to get cold." He held up the box.

"Oh, yeah." She thrust several bills into his hand. "Keep the change."

He grinned. "Thanks. You like rocks, huh?"

"Certain kinds," she agreed absently, rubbing her thumb on the glossy surface.

"Well, enjoy." He lifted his hand in a quick wave and loped back to his truck.

Stacy yanked at the filament. When she had the small stone safely in her palm, her fingers clenched around it. She stepped out on the porch and looked around.

When her gaze finally dropped to the ground, she briefly closed her eyes at what she saw and worried about the pain in her chest. Then she remembered to breathe. She bent down to pick up the gleaming stone in front of her foot. And the one in front of that and the trail of them that led across the small porch, ending in a cluster on the opposite doorstep.

Stacy stood before the door, hope resonating through her body as loudly as the blood pounding in her head.

Mac! It had to be Mac. She lifted her hand to knock on the door when a small, inner voice suggested that it might not be, it might be a serial killer, for heaven's sake. She knocked, anyway, thinking that if it wasn't Mac, she really wouldn't care.

"Come in."

Mac. That rumbly voice couldn't be disguised. Stacy remembered to breathe again and threw open the door. She stood on the threshold, clutching the stones and the pizza, and just stared at him.

Feasted on the sight of him.

He sat on the couch, wearing his straw hat tugged down on his forehead, a light blue shirt with the sleeves rolled up his forearms and slacks. His booted feet were propped on the coffee table, negligently crossed at the ankles. He looked wonderful. He looked tired. And thinner. His dark eyes were all over her.

"You look exhausted, and you've lost weight," he accused.

"I'm sorry."

"You haven't been taking care of yourself."

Stacy shook her head. "I didn't mean that. I mean I'm sorry I left the way I did."

Mac looked down at his hand and flexed his fingers. Fingers that were mostly healed. "You damn well should be. You almost cracked my heart."

"Mine, too," she said, close to tears. "I wanted to call. Every night I started to—"

"Then why the hell didn't you?" His voice was stark.

"I was afraid."

"Of *me?*" He looked at her, appalled.

"Never! Never you," she said shakily. "Never."

"Of what, then?"

"That you might not talk to me. I deserved it, but I couldn't bear it."

He groaned and thumbed the brim of his hat up an inch. "I love you, you crazy woman. I told you that the night before you left. From here to heaven and back, remember? From now until forever. So why *wouldn't* I want to talk to you?"

She sniffed. "I thought you'd never want to hear from me again. And the longer I was gone, the harder it got. I didn't know how to tell you what I was doing, or if you'd care."

"I know everywhere you've been." He recited the cities she'd stayed in as if he were reading a grocery list. "And I cared. Every damned inch of the way, I cared."

Stacy stared at him, her eyes wide with amazement. "But how—"

"Are you going to stand in the door all night, or are you coming in?"

Still staring at him, Stacy reached back and elbowed the door closed. "What are you doing here?"

"Following your orders."

Stacy blinked. "What orders?"

"The ones in your note. You told me to find the woman I need."

She would think about that later, she promised herself, feeling some of the ice in her stomach starting to melt. Dazed, she tried again. "How—"

"Sit down." He lifted his arm as if inviting her to curl next to him, but she dropped in the nearest chair and tried again.

"How—"

Mac exhaled sharply. "I spent about an hour swearing, stomping around the house and promising to throttle you if I ever got my hands on you." And having Maxie stitch his hand. "Then I got on the CB."

Stacy blinked as if she'd never heard the word. "CB?"

"Yeah. That thing in the car you have such fun with? Well, I told every trucker I could reach that Tumbleweed was on the loose again. I also told them she was mine, and if anything happened to her, there'd be hell to pay."

She was astonished. "You did?"

Mac sighed again. "I did. And then it was three whole days before you called in. Three hellish days that seemed like years. What the hell were you doing?"

"Crying." Just remembering, she felt her eyes misting up. "Mac, why are you wearing your hat in here?"

He looked at her, his dark eyes uncertain. "Because you said it was sexy, and I figured I needed all the help I could get."

Stacy gazed at him with her heart in her eyes as tears rolled down her cheeks. Big, fat, hot tears that she couldn't stop. "I don't know what's the matter with me," she wailed. "I've cried more in the past five weeks than I have in my entire life. I just can't seem to—Mac! What are you doing?"

"Guess." Mac scooped her up, crushing her against him as he walked across to the bed. "Someway, somehow, we'll work this out, but right now I have to hold you, make love to you, or I won't really believe that you're here."

He got rid of their clothes and held her tight. "Tell me you want this as much as I do."

"I do. I *do*."

"Good." His voice was a satisfied growl. "We'll try that line again, later. But now..."

They were too starved for the touch of each other to go slowly, to engage in the age-old game of advance and retreat. They clung, their mouths and hands desperately brushing and touching, seeking, comforting.

"Mac, you make me feel like the only woman in the world."

"You are." His voice was tender. "You are."

"Mac, I can't wait!"

"Good."

"Now!"

"Yes! *Yes*." His cry met hers, blending in need and satisfaction, breaking as his body convulsed. And his arms held her as if he would never let her go. Never.

Later, sated and exhausted, he said, "We'll travel, as much and as far as you want."

Stacy smiled and touched her lips to his shoulder. "Not for a while, okay?"

"And if you want to go hunting power places, I'll do it."

"I threw the book away," she confessed. "I'm not sure I really believe that theory. But if it is right, I think I found mine. At our grotto."

He leaned up on his elbow and looked down at her. "As for this inner-woman stuff, I don't understand what you're looking for. Sweetheart, you are more woman than any man ever hopes to find."

Stacy touched her fingers to his lips. "I'll cherish that," she told him. "Forever." She gazed up at him and said slowly, "It's not that I thought I lacked anything, I just wanted to understand what I had."

"And do you?"

"Not completely. But I think that's part of the process. I'll keep learning."

"And what about the excitement you were looking for? The adventure?"

Stacy stared up at him, astounded that he didn't understand. "I found it."

Mac frowned. "Where?"

"In the most unlikely place imaginable," she assured him with a satisfied grin. "In the arms of a rock-solid, dependable man call Gibraltar."

Mac hugged her, holding her tight. Then, determined to get over the rest of the rough ground, he said abruptly, "What about your M.B.A.?"

"It's a piece of paper," she murmured, tracing one of his dark brows with a languid finger. "What about it?"

"It's not the paper I'm worried about. It's what it represents. You've run a big company, for God's sake!"

"I was a workaholic for four solid years," she countered. "I don't ever want to do that again."

"But are you going to be happy living a hundred miles from the nearest big town?" he persisted bleakly.

"I thought about that," she admitted.

"And?"

"I know myself well enough to know that I'll want to keep up with things. How would you like to turn all the ranch paperwork over to me? All the quarterly and annual reports—things like that?"

He looked at her, stunned. "You'd *like* that?"

She nodded, a reminiscent smile curving her lips. "One of my favorite things is keeping the IRS on its toes."

Mac paled. "Now, sweetheart," he began uneasily.

"Mac, darling," she laughed up at him, "I'm *very* good at what I do."

He exhaled sharply. "Okay."

She gave him a quick hug and settled back against him. "There *is* one other thing," she said slowly.

Mac stiffened. "What?"

"I got a good bit of cash as my share of the company, and I'd like to invest some of it in small businesses. It's something I've always wanted to do and never had time. I've seen so many of them go belly-up. Needlessly. Usually because the people lacked experience or basic knowledge. I'd like to find some hardworking entrepreneurs and act as a mentor."

"How are you going to do that from the ranch?"

"Fax machine," she said promptly. "Once the initial interviews are over." Her eyes grew bright with the possibilities. "We'll work it out."

"Yeah." He finally relaxed, pulling her closer. "We'll work it out."

Seconds later Stacy gave him a quick, worried glance. "Mac, what about you? I know I'm not the kind of wife you planned on. Tell me honestly, do you have any regrets?"

Mac gave a shout of laughter. "Regrets? I can see it all now. You'll drive me crazy and probably produce a brood of hellions that will finish the job." He grew serious, studying her tenderly. "And you'll bring me laughter and sunshine and all the love I can handle. No, love. No regrets."

Stacy smiled, a small feminine smile. Then, before satisfaction completely turned her brain to mush, she asked, "Mac? How did you know I was here?"

"Ever since you left, I've had more calls than Maxie or I could keep track of, telling me where you bedded down each night and how you were doing. Big Mama called me three nights ago."

"Oh." She thought about that and finally asked, "Why did you wait so long to come?"

His arm tightened around her. "Because you needed the time. I wanted you, but I wanted you happy."

"Aren't you clever." Her eyes were tender.

"Yep," he said complacently, dropping a swift kiss on the tip of her nose. "By the way, I called your aunt Tabby and told her we were getting married."

Her eyes rounded. "What did she say?"

Mac grinned. "That it was about time. And she hoped our house wasn't furnished, because all the things they took from your place are waiting for you. Oh, uh, one other thing . . ." He hesitated, and Stacy got nervous.

"What?"

"The wedding's set for next Saturday. Your church in Prudence, your mother's dress. The whole town's invited. I'm flying Maxie and the men in for the shindig. That okay?"

Tears filled her eyes, and Stacy covered her face with her hands. "Oh, damn, I'm going to cry again."

Mac grinned. "Is that a *yes?*"

"Yes!"

"Sweetheart?

"What?"

"Do you love me?"

"Yes."

"And you'll be happy living on the ranch?"

"Yes."

Figuring he was on a roll, Mac asked, "And you're starved for my body and want to make love again?"

"Yes, you crazy man. Oh, *yes!*"

* * * * *

**Relive the romance...
Harlequin and Silhouette
are proud to present**

by Request™

A program of collections of three complete novels by the most requested authors with the most requested themes. Be sure to look for one volume each month with three complete novels by top name authors.

In January: **WESTERN LOVING**   Susan Fox
                                    JoAnn Ross
                                    Barbara Kaye

Loving a cowboy is easy—taming him isn't!

In February: **LOVER, COME BACK!**   Diana Palmer
                                        Lisa Jackson
                                        Patricia Gardner Evans

It was over so long ago—yet now they're calling, "Lover, Come Back!"

In March: **TEMPERATURE RISING**   JoAnn Ross
                                      Tess Gerritsen
                                      Jacqueline Diamond

Falling in love—just what the doctor ordered!

Available at your favorite retail outlet.

REQ-G3

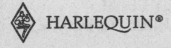

He staked his claim...

HONOR BOUND

by
New York Times
Bestselling Author

Sandra Brown

previously published under the pseudonym Erin St. Claire

As Aislinn Andrews opened her mouth to scream, a hard
hand clamped over her face and she found herself face-
to-face with Lucas Greywolf, a lean, lethal-looking
Navajo and escaped convict who swore he wouldn't hurt
her— *if* she helped him.

Look for HONOR BOUND at your favorite
retail outlet this January.

Only from...

Silhouette

where passion lives. SBHB

**Fifty red-blooded, white-hot, true-blue hunks
from every State in the Union!**

Look for MEN MADE IN AMERICA! Written by some
of our most poplar authors, these stories feature fifty of
the strongest, sexiest men, each from a different state in
the union!

Two titles available every other month at your favorite
retail outlet.

In January, look for:

DREAM COME TRUE by Ann Major (Florida)
WAY OF THE WILLOW by Linda Shaw (Georgia)

In March, look for:

TANGLED LIES by Anne Stuart (Hawaii)
ROGUE'S VALLEY by Kathleen Creighton (Idaho)

You won't be able to resist MEN MADE IN AMERICA!

SILHOUETTE.... Where Passion Lives

Don't miss these Silhouette favorites by some of our most popular authors!
And now, you can receive a discount by ordering two or more titles!

Silhouette Desire®

#05751	THE MAN WITH THE MIDNIGHT EYES BJ James	$2.89	☐
#05763	THE COWBOY Cait London	$2.89	☐
#05774	TENNESSEE WALTZ Jackie Merritt	$2.89	☐
#05779	THE RANCHER AND THE RUNAWAY BRIDE Joan Johnston	$2.89	☐

Silhouette Intimate Moments®

#07417	WOLF AND THE ANGEL Kathleen Creighton	$3.29	☐
#07480	DIAMOND WILLOW Kathleen Eagle	$3.39	☐
#07486	MEMORIES OF LAURA Marilyn Pappano	$3.39	☐
#07493	QUINN EISLEY'S WAR Patricia Gardner Evans	$3.39	☐

Silhouette Shadows®

#27003	STRANGER IN THE MIST Lee Karr	$3.50	☐
#27007	FLASHBACK Terri Herrington	$3.50	☐
#27009	BREAK THE NIGHT Anne Stuart	$3.50	☐
#27012	DARK ENCHANTMENT Jane Toombs	$3.50	☐

Silhouette Special Edition®

#09754	THERE AND NOW Linda Lael Miller	$3.39	☐
#09770	FATHER: UNKNOWN Andrea Edwards	$3.39	☐
#09791	THE CAT THAT LIVED ON PARK AVENUE Tracy Sinclair	$3.39	☐
#09811	HE'S THE RICH BOY Lisa Jackson	$3.39	☐

Silhouette Romance®

#08893	LETTERS FROM HOME Toni Collins	$2.69	☐
#08915	NEW YEAR'S BABY Stella Bagwell	$2.69	☐
#08927	THE PURSUIT OF HAPPINESS Anne Peters	$2.69	☐
#08952	INSTANT FATHER Lucy Gordon	$2.75	☐

	AMOUNT	$ _____
DEDUCT:	10% DISCOUNT FOR 2+ BOOKS	$ _____
	POSTAGE & HANDLING	$ _____
	($1.00 for one book, 50¢ for each additional)	
	APPLICABLE TAXES*	$ _____
	TOTAL PAYABLE	$ _____
	(check or money order—please do not send cash)	

To order, complete this form and send it, along with a check or money order for the total above, payable to Silhouette Books, to: *In the U.S.*: 3010 Walden Avenue, P.O. Box 9077, Buffalo, NY 14269-9077; *In Canada*: P.O. Box 636, Fort Erie, Ontario, L2A 5X3.

Name: _____

Address: _____ City: _____

State/Prov.: _____ Zip/Postal Code: _____

*New York residents remit applicable sales taxes.
Canadian residents remit applicable GST and provincial taxes.

SBACK-OD